THE KINGDOM OF NO WORRIES

OTHER BOOKS BY
PHILIP ROY

*Stealth of the Ninja* (2017)

*Mouse Vacation* (2016)

*Mouse Pet* (2015)

*Eco Warrior* (2015)

*Jellybean Mouse* (2014)

*Mouse Tales* (2014)

*Me & Mr. Bell* (2013)

*Seas of South Africa* (2013)

*Frères de sang à Louisbourg* (2013)

*Blood Brothers in Louisbourg* (2012)

*Outlaw in India* (2012)

*Ghosts of the Pacific* (2011)

*River Odyssey* (2010)

*Journey to Atlantis* (2009)

*Submarine Outlaw* (2008)

# The Kingdom
# of No Worries

Philip Roy

RONSDALE PRESS

THE KINGDOM OF NO WORRIES
Copyright © 2017 Philip Roy

RONSDALE PRESS
3350 West 21st Avenue, Vancouver, B.C., Canada V6S 1G7
www.ronsdalepress.com

Typesetting: Julie Cochrane, in Minion 12 pt on 18
Cover Art & Design: Elisa Gutiérrez
Paper: 70 lb. Rolland Opaque Smooth Natural (FSC)—100% post-consumer
    waste, totally chlorine-free and acid-free

Ronsdale Press wishes to thank the following for their support of its publishing program: the Canada Council for the Arts, the Government of Canada through the Canada Book Fund, the British Columbia Arts Council, and the Province of British Columbia through the British Columbia Book Publishing Tax Credit program.

**Library and Archives Canada Cataloguing in Publication**

Roy, Philip, 1960–, author
    The kingdom of no worries / Philip Roy. — First edition.

Issued in print and electronic formats.
ISBN 978-1-55380-511-3 (softcover)
ISBN 978-1-55380-512-0 (ebook) / ISBN 978-1-55380-513-7 (pdf)

    I. Title.

PS8635.O91144K54 2017    jC813'.6    C2017-902600-3    C2017-902601-1

At Ronsdale Press we are committed to protecting the environment. To this end we are working with Canopy and printers to phase out our use of paper produced from ancient forests. This book is one step towards that goal.

Printed in Canada by Marquis Printing, Quebec

*for the newest
young Canadians*

# ACKNOWLEDGEMENTS

This book was inspired by conversations I have had with many students in schools in and around the Greater Toronto Area. For over a generation I have witnessed the construction and expansion of neighbourhoods that now house millions of people who have come to Canada from around the world. I could not have guessed back then, when the excavators were clearing the land, that the residents to fill those neighbourhoods would be the brilliant young faces I now meet in the schools. Canada is a model for the world. I can't imagine any other place where global vision is not just an aspiration but a harmonious day-to-day reality, as in these neighbourhoods. I feel deeply fortunate to have the opportunity to work within this environment, and I am grateful to these young Canadians for their inspiration and wondrous ideas.

I would like to acknowledge the Canada Council for the Arts for its support in the creation of this book. I wish also to thank Ronsdale for its continued publication of my projects, and also my incredible wife, Leila; my mother, Ellen; my sisters, Angela and Estelle; my fabulous kids: Julia, Petra, Thomas, Julian, and Eva; and my dearest friends: Chris, Natasha, and Chiara. No author was ever blessed with more affectionate support.

"So we must lay another command on our guardians: they are to take all possible care that the state neither shall be too small nor yet one that seems great but has no unity . . . We must watch them, I think, at every age and see . . . that they must do what is best for the community . . ."

— PLATO, *The Republic*

# Chapter 1

ONCE UPON A TIME nobody owned anything. People ran around naked and the world was wonderful and free.

Now, everything is owned by *somebody*: some are filthy rich, and some are dirt poor; some live in gigantic mansions, and some sleep on the sidewalk. How did that happen? Why can't I go out in the woods and build my own castle? What would happen if I did, would they put me in jail? Who gives them the right to do that?

And who's *they*, anyway?

This question jumps out of me on the last day of school, while Mom makes my lunch and Dad grinds coffee.

"Who owns the land?"

They both turn and stare at me, but Mom just smiles, and Dad's still waking up. I feel a hand come down on my shoulder.

"I'm glad you asked," says Merilee, my sister.

*No!*

Merilee's just three years older but you would guess she was a lot older than that. She's a bookworm, an A+ student, and a political activist. She writes long letters to politicians and they write back. They always start out by thanking her for her sharp insight and end by asking for money. Once, a politician even asked her to join his re-election committee, but she turned him down because he was too conservative. They don't have a clue that she's only fifteen years old.

Dad calls Merilee a "*paragon* of conscience," which sounds like a flying dinosaur to me. Mom says that when she was pregnant with Merilee she ate spinach, broccoli, and pine nuts, took long walks in nature, listened to Mozart, and read books. When she was pregnant with me she ate only mac and cheese, Skittles, pop, and slouched on the sofa in front of the soaps. That explains my cravings for junk food.

Merilee doesn't have a lot of time for me usually, unless I ask a question about the world, such as . . . "Why do people care so much about what other people wear, like . . . hijabs, burkas, and things like that?" or "Why can't countries just get rid of their dictators if they don't like them?" Then she'll follow me around all day long answering one simple question. She'll start slowly, for my sake, but will pick up speed after a while, especially if I appear to lose interest, and will go on and on if I try to run away, and even follow me into my tree fort in the backyard answering one measly question, which by then I won't even remember, and will wish I had never asked, and will promise myself never to ask again. But sometimes a question will slip out when I'm not paying attention, like now.

I look up at Dad, hoping he'll answer first, but he won't speak until he's had his first sip of coffee. I look at Mom, but she just keeps smiling. She never interrupts Merilee.

"There's crown land, and there's private land," Merilee says as she sits down and stares into my face. I look up at the clock.

"I have to get to school."

"Crown land is owned by the province. Private land is owned by individuals, or companies."

"I have to go pee."

"It might surprise you to know that eighty-five percent of the land in Ontario is owned by the Crown."

I start to get up. She digs her fingers into my shoulder, which is probably what a mouse feels like when it is carried away by an owl. I sit back down.

"Sometimes you can rent or buy land from the Crown, but you need special permission from the Ministry of Natural Resources, because land is considered a resource, just like forests and rivers and mines."

I'm starting to feel sleepy. I wonder if I can stay home sick today. No, my friends and I have agreed to meet after school to discuss our plans for the summer, which just means epic sessions of video games, movies, and skateboarding. Still, it has to be planned out, which also happens to be a good excuse for an epic junk-food pig-out.

"Once someone buys land and is given legal title to it, they, or their heirs, hold it in perpetuity." Merilee tosses her hair as if she's in a shampoo commercial. "On the other hand, people sometimes just lease land, as from the Crown, in which case the ownership reverts to the Crown once the lease runs out. But land leases often run for a hundred years . . ."

I'm starting to zone out, but I hear Merilee use the

word *perpetuity*, which I'm pretty sure is a pot that old geezers spit chewing tobacco into. I wonder if you can pee into a *perpetuity*. I look down at the floor—we don't have one of those. I look up at Dad. He's standing over the coffee maker with his hand on the kettle and no water coming out. He has daydreamed himself into a trance. That's something I inherited from him. I have yet to discover any original traits within myself.

Merilee senses I'm not paying attention, so she picks up the pace. Her voice drifts in and out of the window with the breeze. My sister has two friends who are exactly like her: Mehra and Marcie. Dad calls them "the Three Fates." If you sit close to them in the school cafeteria when they are brainstorming, your head will explode.

". . . is owned by the Huron Nation. In fact, our whole city is legally owned by the Huron Nation . . ."

"*What . . ?*"

I raise my head. For a second, I think I hear something actually interesting. I turn and look into the blindingly smart eyes of my sister. "What? The city of Briffin?"

Merilee is so unused to me asking a question once she's on a roll, she looks a little confused, like a lizard that has just stumbled upon a sleeping bug. "Yes. Legally, they own it. But . . . they can't possess it."

"Why not?"

"Because the treaties are contested. And there's conflicting evidence, at least that's what the Crown lawyers will tell you. The whole thing is so deeply mired in legal technicalities it would probably take a hundred years to sort it out through the courts. But mostly it's because we're living here, and it's too expensive to move a city."

"Wow. That's interesting." I really mean it. Merilee nods her head, stands up, and pours herself a bowl of cereal. She looks pleased. I wait for her to begin again but she doesn't. She starts eating her cereal. I can't believe it. I have just learned a most valuable lesson: to escape Merilee all you have to do is show a little interest.

# Chapter 2

A LITTLE WHILE LATER, I'm in the car with Dad on my way to school. Dad's a civil engineer for the city. He's one of the folks who decide where to dig ditches, tear up roads, lay down sewer pipes, and pour sidewalks. But it seems to me that they always tear up more than they lay down, and every time we drive through the city I sink deeper into my seat because I figure people know it's our fault they're sitting in traffic. And it doesn't help that Dad yells out the window, "Hey, Joe! Bart! Ted! Nice diggin', boys!" They wave but never smile. Only

Dad does, 'cause he's the only one who sees the beauty in a ripped-up street.

We drive along the river past the shiny brand new Hindu temple, the Mormon church with the golden trumpeter on the roof, the yellow brick Catholic church, the grey brick Anglican church, the white brick Presbyterian church, the Bank of Ontario, the Briffin Public Library, the Better-life Insurance Co., the Finer-life Insurance Co., the Second-chance car dealership, and the red brick post office. Dad's talking, ". . . blah, blah, blah . . ." but I'm lost in thought. I'm wondering what all this land looked like before these buildings were here. Were there First Nations wigwams? Were there long-houses? I turn towards the river, and there . . . I see it.

"Dad?"

". . . blah, blah, blah . . . Yeah?"

"What's that piece of land out there?"

"Where?"

"There. In the middle of the river."

He looks over. "That? Well, that's been growing ever since the new treatment plant went in. We've been redirecting part of the river to clean and recycle it. It reconnects downstream. You know, I told you all about it last year. Remember? We had a picnic down there where the rivers come together again."

I remember the picnic but have no idea why we were there, which doesn't mean that he didn't tell me.

"It's as big as a soccer field."

"Yup."

"And it wasn't there before?"

"Nope."

"So . . . who owns it?"

"What?"

"Who owns it?"

"Who owns it?" We pull up to a traffic light and Dad twists around to take a closer look. "Nobody owns it, I suppose."

"Nobody owns it?"

"No. I don't see how anybody could own it. It didn't exist until now."

"Wow. That's cool."

"Yeah, but it's just a flat stretch of sand and rock. Nobody could build there or live there; it's in the middle of the river. Besides, there's an old dam in the Upper Huronia River District, and if they ever open it up, as they sometimes do, the river will swell twice its size, and that piece of land will disappear quicker than you can say 'lickety-split.'"

"Oh. When was the last time they opened the dam?"

"Ahhh . . . 1973."

"So it's safe to assume they won't open it anytime soon."

"I wouldn't say that. Okay. Here we are. Behave yourself, Billy. Don't get thrown out of school on the last day."

"I won't. Thanks, Dad."

I trudge inside the school, listen to the end-of-the-year speeches, the final projects, the sports teams' feats, and the programs they offer to try to trick kids into staying in school year round, and the day passes like a rainy day at the fall fair when the rides aren't open. Then I meet up with Sami and Charlie, and we go out the front door together into the glowing sunshine, and we feel like we own the whole world.

Sami's my best friend. He moved to Canada three years ago from Abu Dhabi, and before that he lived in Lebanon. His family were refugees when they first came to Canada. We're the same age but he's three inches taller. Sami's got a face like a wrestler, and a high voice like a girl's. He spends all his time playing video games but avoids going into battle. He likes dressing up warriors with armour and weapons, and then goes out of his way to avoid getting blood on them. He'll spend weeks on a quest for a single weapon or piece of armour, but the thought of actually hurting someone bothers him too much to enjoy the fighting. I've never seen him angry. I'm not sure I would want to. I think he carries a lot of sadness inside, and if it ever came out as anger, he might be like the Incredible Hulk.

Sami spends most of his time gaming because there's no one at home to tell him not to. But he can also quote lines from famous books, which shows that he reads a lot, though I don't know where he gets the time, unless he doesn't sleep. He wants to be a hotshot lawyer when he grows up, like his dad, but he's always singing songs from Disney movies like *The Lion King* or *The Little Mermaid* and can impersonate movie stars, so I don't know, I think maybe he should be an actor or a filmmaker. He wants to be a lawyer because his dad is a lawyer, and he adores his dad, even though he never gets to see him. I like Sami because he's the most loyal friend you could ever find. He would never betray you, even if he were strapped down in a torturer's chair.

My other best friend is Charlie. We were born in the same hospital just three months apart, but most people think Charlie is from China because his parents are from China, and he doesn't speak much, so they assume he can't speak English. Charlie is fun to hang around with, even though he's kind of gloomy. Actually, he's very gloomy, but it's a witty kind of gloomy that makes you laugh. When he's focusing on something, he gets an angry look on his face, but it's just a look. Like Sami, he's loyal, but you wouldn't know it to listen to him. You'd think that Charlie doesn't like anybody or anything, but it's just that he's so gloomy about it. I don't even remember how we became friends. We went to the same school right from the beginning, and just sort of gravitated towards each other over the years. He says he wants to be a brain surgeon or a heart surgeon or a bone doctor, whichever one makes the most money.

Charlie is thin, and a little shorter than me. He has one special talent: he can dance like Michael Jackson. Along with signed posters on his wall—I don't believe Michael Jackson actually signed them—he keeps an MJ costume, with white sparkly gloves and shiny black shoes. Charlie can do a whole MJ routine, including the moonwalk, when no one's watching. He calls me Billie-Jean, after one of MJ's best songs.

SAMI: "Guys. Let's go to my place and play *Demon Revival X*; there's nobody home."

CHARLIE: "There's never anybody home, Sami. Your place is a tomb. Let's grab some candy and go to the park. It's nice outside."

ME: "Actually, guys, I want to show you something."

CHARLIE: "What?"

ME: "Something special."

SAMI: "What?"

ME: "You have to see it."

SAMI: "No, you have to tell us."

ME: "You have to see it. Come on, it's not far."

CHARLIE: "*Where* is it?"

Charlie falls apart if he has to walk anywhere he doesn't want to go.

ME: "It's really close."

SAMI: "Where's close?"

ME: "The river."

SAMI: "The *river*? What's at the river, a dead fish?"

CHARLIE: "I don't wanna see a dead fish."

ME: "It's not a dead fish. It's special. Trust me, you'll be impressed."

They stare at me with untrusting faces but follow me down to the river. Charlie whines all the way.

CHARLIE: "Carry me, Billie-Jean. Carry me. Carry me. Carry me, Billie-Jean . . ."

ME: "Shut up, Charlie!"

SAMI: "Okay. There's the river. Where's the surprise?"

ME: "There."

SAMI: "Where?"

ME: "Right there."

SAMI: "What, that? That's a swamp. What's so exciting about a swamp?"

ME: "It's not a swamp. It's land."

SAMI: "Okay. So . . ?"

ME: "It doesn't belong to anybody."

When Sami frowns, his forehead reaches down to the top of his nose, his lips curl up, and his face looks like a baloney sandwich. Charlie's face does the opposite; his eyes open wide and his ears go back like a chihuahua.

CHARLIE: "You mean . . . it doesn't belong to *anybody*?"

ME: "That's right."

SAMI: "You mean . . . *nobody*?"

ME: "Nobody."

CHARLIE: "You mean . . . it's for the taking?"

# Chapter 3

WE'RE SITTING IN my tree fort in the backyard. It's getting dark. Over a junk-food feast we have talked ourselves into the creation of our own country. We have to work out a few details, but we've basically decided to take possession of the land in the river before anyone else does. We figure it can become an entirely new country, independent and free, governed by the laws we will make. We will devote our summer to creating those laws; we just can't agree on what sort of country it should be. I think it should be a democracy, Charlie wants an aristocracy, and Sami wants a kingdom. The problem is: none of us knows for sure what those are. We have a lot to learn, and fast.

SAMI: "Well, that's ironic."

ME: "What's ironic?"

SAMI: "Here we are on the last day of school, with the freedom we've been waiting for all year, and now that we've got it, all we want to do is study."

CHARLIE: "That's depressing."

SAMI: "We'll probably learn more than we ever learned in school."

CHARLIE: "We'll probably learn more than our teachers."

ME: "I don't care; I just want that land."

CHARLIE: "I feel sick."

ME: "You ate too much candy."

CHARLIE: "No, I didn't."

ME: "We all did. Where's that bag of Halloween candy that I kept under my bed all year?"

CHARLIE: "You kept it under your bed?"

ME: "Yeah."

CHARLIE: "With spiders and silverfish and earwigs?"

ME: "Yeah. There are wrappers on the candy. Where's the bag?"

SAMI: "It's under the chips bowl."

ME: "No, it isn't."

SAMI: "It was before. Look again."

ME: "I just did. It's not there."

SAMI: "It couldn't disappear into thin air."

CHARLIE: "I ate it."

ME: "You ate the whole *bag*?"

CHARLIE: "I have a high metabolism."

ME: "There were other things in that bag, Charlie. You'd better give me back the crayons and eraser."

CHARLIE: "Crayons and eraser? *I ate crayons and an eraser?*"

SAMI: "They won't hurt you."

CHARLIE: "Yes, they will! You guys better rush me to the hospital."

ME: "No way! You're fine. They'll pass through you."

CHARLIE: "No, they won't. They'll clog my arteries and give me a heart attack. We have to go to the hospital."

ME: "How could you eat crayons and an eraser, Charlie? Didn't you notice?"

CHARLIE: "We were so busy talking. I was distracted."

ME: "I think I would know when I was eating an eraser."

SAMI: "It's just wax and rubber, Charlie. The eraser is probably even good for your arteries."

CHARLIE: "They're gonna kill me. I'm feeling really sick now. You guys have to take me to the hospital."

ME: "Actually, I just remembered there were no crayons or eraser in that bag; I made a mistake."

CHARLIE: "You're lying."

ME: "No, I'm not. Really."

CHARLIE: "Now you're lying about lying."

ME: "Charlie . . ."

CHARLIE: "We have to go to the hospital right now. Go ask your dad to drive us."

ME: "Charlie, there were no crayons or eraser in that bag. I just made a mistake."

SAMI: "Guys, can we get on with making our own country now?"

CHARLIE: "I have to throw up."

ME: "Don't throw up in here!"

CHARLIE: *Burrrrrrrrrrrrrrp!*

ME: "What was that?"

SAMI: "I think it was a crayon burp."

CHARLIE: "Actually . . . I feel better now."

SAMI: "Good. Can we get on with it?"

ME: "We have to have a democracy, guys, so everyone can vote."

CHARLIE: "But I want an aristocracy."

ME: "Charlie, an aristocracy is just for rich people."

CHARLIE: "I know. That's what I like about it. If we make an aristocracy we'll be rich."

ME: "It doesn't work like that."

CHARLIE: "Yes, it does."

ME: "No, it doesn't."

SAMI: "Guys, democracies and aristocracies aren't very special. Kingdoms are special. I think it should be a kingdom."

ME: "A kingdom has to have a king, Sami."

SAMI: "So?"

ME: "There are three of us."

CHARLIE: "In case you haven't noticed."

SAMI: "We'll take turns."

ME: "Take turns being king?"

SAMI: "Why not?"

CHARLIE: "First! I called first."

ME: "Can it be a democracy and a kingdom at the same time?"

CHARLIE: "Nope."

SAMI: "I don't know. Why don't you ask Merilee? She'll know."

ME: "Okay."

CHARLIE: "We could set up an amusement park, and charge people for attendance."

SAMI: "Pretty small amusement park."

CHARLIE: "Not if we build straight up, like in Hong Kong."

SAMI: "I think we should open a casino."

ME: "You can't just open a casino."

CHARLIE: "We can do whatever we want in our own country."

SAMI: "That's true."

ME: "But how do we declare it a country?"

SAMI: "We need a flag. We need to stick it in the ground. I'll make one."

ME: "Okay."

CHARLIE: "We'll need a national anthem. Every country has one. I'll write one."

ME: "Okay."

SAMI: "We'll need a standing army."

ME: "What's a standing army?"

SAMI: "I don't know; it's an army."

ME: "We'll have to be the army for now. We can hire real soldiers later."

CHARLIE: "What about weapons?"

ME: "I can bring my pellet gun."

SAMI: "I can bring my Swiss Army knife."

CHARLIE: "I can bring a plunger."

ME: "A *plunger*?"

CHARLIE: "People are afraid of plungers. You'd be surprised."

ME: "Okay. What else do we need?"

SAMI: "A political system."

ME: "Oh, boy. We'd better write this down."

CHARLIE: "Who are we going to let in?"

SAMI: "Everyone."

CHARLIE: "Even people with weird religions?"

SAMI: "It doesn't matter what religion you have."

CHARLIE: "But what about the ones who come to your door to brainwash you into giving them all your money?"

SAMI: "We don't have to join their church just because they come to our country, Charlie."

CHARLIE: "What about neo-Nazis?"

ME: "No way! That's not a religion; that's a political group. They're practically terrorists. No terrorists are allowed."

SAMI: "Definitely no terrorists."

CHARLIE: "What about genders?"

ME: "What about them?"

CHARLIE: "Which ones will we let in?"

SAMI: "All of them. It doesn't matter what your gender is."

CHARLIE: "How many are there?"

ME: "I don't know, lots."

SAMI: "All genders are welcome. Our country is completely open and tolerant. We want to set an example for the world."

ME: "That's right. An example for the world."

CHARLIE: "What are we going to call it?"

ME: "Call what?"

CHARLIE: "Our country."

SAMI: "*Hakuna matata.*"

ME: "We can't. That's copyrighted."

CHARLIE: "Which means . . ?"

ME: "Which means we can't use it or we'll get sued."

CHARLIE: "What does *hakuna matata* mean anyway?"

SAMI: "Didn't you watch *The Lion King*?"

CHARLIE: "Yeah, like six years ago."

SAMI: "You should watch it again. It's only the greatest movie ever made. It means 'no worries.'"

ME: "The Kingdom of No Worries?"

SAMI: "Yeah. *The Kingdom of No Worries*. That's awesome."

CHARLIE: "Sounds good to me. I've got to go home."

ME: "I've got to go inside."

SAMI: "I've got to go to the bathroom."

ME: "Go by the fence."

SAMI: "No, I've got to go to the *bathroom*."

ME: "Oh. You'd better go home."

CHARLIE: "Let's meet tomorrow after we've looked all this stuff up."

ME: "Okay."

SAMI: "Okay."

# Chapter 4

MERILEE'S MEETING MEHRA and Marcie and they're going to school. They are the ones who take the summer programs that would prematurely end the lives of people like Sami, Charlie, and me. They'd have to drag us into the school kicking and screaming and scratching at the bricks with bleeding fingers. Then they'd have to take us out in coffins. But the Three Fates go willingly, which just shows how there are completely different species amongst human beings, even in the same family.

I appear at the open bathroom door, where Merilee is brushing her teeth and cleaning her face. Merilee doesn't wear makeup because it's just a clever marketing scheme to keep women enslaved. I feel like telling her that wearing her hair up like that makes her look older than her teachers. I open my mouth, but no words come out. She turns and looks down at me like a bird with a long sharp beak. "Yes?"

"I have a couple of questions."

She frowns. She is suspicious. "What? It's summer. Why aren't you out killing frogs somewhere?"

"I don't kill frogs."

"What sort of questions? If this is about your wee-wee, you'd better ask Dad, not me."

"It's not about that. This is serious."

"I have to make lunch. Follow me."

I follow her into the kitchen. I have a terrible feeling that I am supposed to be outside and not come back inside until the summer is over, that I am getting myself into something I might deeply regret, and yet I know we cannot move forward with our country if we don't have more information. I am also wondering why I have gone to school all these years and I don't know anything about anything.

"Okay. Shoot."

I look down at the paper in my hand where I scribbled a bunch of questions. "What's the difference between a democracy and a kingdom?"

Merilee turns her beak towards me again. She's still suspicious.

"Hmmm. A democracy is a form of government based upon an assumption of equality for everyone. Everyone is entitled to vote, and the elected government is beholden to the people. A kingdom is not a form of government; it's a form of state, which is typically ruled by a monarchy, which is a form of government, essentially an exploitative form of government in which everything is owned by the ruling monarch, and all of the citizens are subjects, subject to the ruler's whims, taxes, punishments, etc. But a lot of monarchies these days are constitutional monarchies, in which case the king or queen is reduced to a figurehead without real power, and the monarchy is basically a democracy under a different name. Why do you ask?"

"Because we found some new land and we want to make it our own country, but we haven't decided yet what form of government we want, except that Sami wants it to be a kingdom."

Merilee shakes her head. "They'll throw you in jail."

"Who will?"

"The police, acting on behalf of the city. Governments don't take kindly to anarchy."

"What's *anarchy*?"

"Intentional disobedience. Look, I've got to get to school. Come here."

I follow her back upstairs into her room. The walls are lined with bookshelves. Books are open on the desk, the floor, and the windowsills. It doesn't look like a bedroom at all, but the heart of a jungle, where all the hanging vines and plants are books strung together, and books rise out of the moss like ferns. In one corner is a small bed, hiding beneath open books. It reminds me of a picture I saw in *National Geographic* magazine of a WWII airplane that went down on an island in the Pacific. The plane was so buried beneath coconut crabs, spiders, and snakes, you could hardly tell what it was.

Merilee goes to one bookshelf, pulls down a dull grey book and hands it to me. "Read this. It will give you the answers you are looking for." Then she goes out the door.

I turn the book over in my hands. I have only ever seen books like this in museums, or used as doorstoppers, or to hold up wobbly picnic tables. I didn't know people actually read them. The cover is too worn to make out the title, so I open it and look inside. It is *The Republic* by Plato. I turn a page and stare at the table of contents. I start to get that dizzy feeling like I am going to fall asleep, but a couple of lines catch my eye. "*Selection of Rulers . . . The Philosopher King . . . Timocracy . . . Democracy and the Democratic Man . . . Oligarchy . . . Plutocracy . . . Despotism . . .*"

I can't help feeling I have stumbled upon a book of secrets. On one hand, the book is completely unreadable. The words look like the names of bugs that never made it onto the scientific classification charts. On the other hand, I have a sneaky feeling that it holds the secret to taking ownership of that piece of land. I feel a bit like Aladdin; all I have to do is rub the lamp . . . or, well, read the book.

I meet Sami and Charlie at the river. Sami's carrying a green folder under his arm. Charlie holds a crumpled piece of paper in his hand. It looks like a candy wrapper. I'm carrying a pole and shovel in my hands, and the book in my backpack. We come together without a word, sit down and stare at the river, and don't speak for at least five minutes. I think we are nervous. Each is waiting for the other to say the words that will commit us for life to this sandy patch of ground surrounded by lazily flowing water.

Finally, Charlie breaks the silence.

CHARLIE: "What's in your pack?"

ME: "A book."

SAMI: "What book?"

ME: "*The Republic.* By Plato. It's got our answers in it. Merilee said so."

CHARLIE: "Did you read it?"

ME: "I opened it. It's pretty dense. It's mostly a conversation between these two guys, but they're talking about all the stuff we're talking about. So far they've said that a king has to be a philosopher."

CHARLIE: "A philosopher? Why does a king have to be a philosopher?"

ME: "I don't know. I think they just mean he's supposed to be wise."

CHARLIE: "Oh."

SAMI: "I looked up countries inside other countries on the net and printed it up. It's really cool. Look. Here's Lesotho. It's a country inside South Africa. It's a kingdom, too, and it's a democracy . . . sort of."

ME: "That's great."

SAMI: "And here's San Marino. It's in Italy. It's a democracy, too. And there's Monaco, in France. It's a constitutional monarchy; and Vatican City, in Italy."

ME: "Vatican City? Isn't that where the Pope lives?"

SAMI: "Yeah."

ME: "And that's a country?"

SAMI: "Yup."

ME: "But isn't it just a city inside another city?"

SAMI: "Yup."

ME: "But it's a country?"

SAMI: "Yeah."

CHARLIE: "I don't think Vatican City is a democracy. I think there's only one person there who can vote: the Pope."

ME: "That's okay. Not every place has to be a democracy. If the Kingdom of Lesotho can be a democracy, then the Kingdom of No Worries can be a democracy, too."

SAMI: "That's right."

ME: "Good work, Sami. What did you bring, Charlie?"

CHARLIE: "This."

He unfolds the wrapper.

ME: "What's that?"

CHARLIE: "Our anthem."

SAMI: "Really? Awesome."

ME: "You actually wrote an anthem?"

CHARLIE: "Yes."

ME: "That's awesome!"

SAMI: "Let's hear it."

Charlie jumps up and gets into his MJ pose.

CHARLIE: "Okay. It goes to the music of 'Billie Jean.'"

ME: "Wait! We can't use that, Charlie. It's copyrighted."

CHARLIE: "No, it's okay. I made up new words."

ME: "Yeah, but the *music* is copyrighted. We'll get sued."

SAMI: "We can't get sued in our own country."

ME: "Oh, yeah. Okay. Let's hear it."

Charlie flattens his hand against his belly, and tilts his head forward as if he's wearing a hat. Then he takes off the hat and throws it onto an imaginary stage. We have to listen carefully, because the words come out fast.

*Oooom . . . pah . . . oooom . . . pah . . .*
*Oooom . . . pah . . . oooom . . . pah . . .*
*It was more like a coun/try, than a river swamp*
*We said we like it but it must be, a de/mo/cra/cy*
*With a king/and a flag/and a vote*
*We said a de/mo/cra/cy . . . with a king/and a*
   *flag/and a vote.*

*They said the land was not owned by/anyone else*
*We thought we'd claim it/a country/of all our own*
*With a king/and a flag/and a vote.*

*People always told us/be careful what you wish for*
*And don't go around/wasting all of your time*
*And teachers always told us/be careful not to try*
*And be careful what you don't do/'cause life will*
     *pass you by.*

*The River King/dom of No Worries*
*It's just a place/we dream for a de/mo/cra/cy*
*But the river holds the key*
*We dream a de/mo/cra/cy, but the river holds the key.*

*The River King/dom of No Worries*
*It's just a place/we dream for a de/mo/cra/cy*
*But the river holds the key*
*We dream a de/mo/cra/cy, but the river holds the key.*

CHARLIE: "That's the chorus. I only have two verses so far, and the bridge."

ME: "It's awesome, Charlie. It's really awesome."

CHARLIE: "Thanks. It's kind of hard to moonwalk on the grass."

SAMI: "It's so cool, Charlie. MJ would be impressed."

CHARLIE: "Thanks."

ME: "Will everyone have to learn the words?"

CHARLIE: "Of course. Just like the Canadian anthem."

ME: "Yeah, I guess so. But what about the dance moves?"

SAMI: "No way. Most people can't dance. They just have to learn the words."

CHARLIE: "I think they should learn the dance moves, too."

ME: "It's too hard, Charlie. Not everybody can dance like you. We don't want to discourage people from joining our country."

SAMI: "That's right."

CHARLIE: "Yeah, okay."

Charlie sits back down and the three of us just stare at our country for a long time.

ME: "We should probably go over there and see what it's like, eh?"

SAMI: "Definitely."

CHARLIE: "I can't swim."

ME: "You can't swim? But you took all those swimming lessons."

CHARLIE: "I know, but I can't swim."

ME: "Then we'll have to carry you."

CHARLIE: "Okay. That sounds good."

SAMI: "Are you sure you can't swim, Charlie?"

CHARLIE: "I can't! Honest. Do you want me to drown?"

Sami and I look at Charlie suspiciously.

CHARLIE: "You guys have to carry me."

SAMI: "Don't be so smug about it, Charlie. We only have to keep your head above water, you know. We can drag the rest of you through the river."

CHARLIE: "If we're going to take turns being king, then I should go first. That way, when you guys carry me over, you'll be carrying over the first king, just like in ancient times when kings were carried around in royal chairs. I think we should find a chair."

ME: "No way! We're not carrying you over in a chair, Charlie. We're kings, too, you know."

CHARLIE: "Yeah, but I'm the first king. I really think we should find a chair."

SAMI: "Where would we find a chair, Charlie? We're going to drag you through the river. Be prepared to get wet."

# Chapter 5

SAMI CARRIES CHARLIE on his shoulders, I carry the pole and shovel, and we cross the river. It's an historic moment. Sami's got our new flag in his backpack, but we haven't seen it yet.

CHARLIE: "Don't drop me."

SAMI: "I won't drop you. Stop wiggling!"

CHARLIE: "I can't help it; your strap is invading my crack."

SAMI: "Stop wiggling! You're making me lose my balance."

The river rises to our necks, forcing Charlie onto Sami's head, like a squirrel on top of a bird feeder. There may be shallower spots, but we haven't found them yet. It's extremely exciting to take the last few steps out of the river and set foot upon our own brand new country. As soon as Charlie jumps down from Sami's shoulders, we declare all together: "We claim this land in the name of democracy, and hereby call it the Kingdom of No Worries."

Our country is flat, bald, and sandy, but it feels so good beneath our feet. It's long and narrow, but you can lie down on it and stare up at the clouds, which we do, and at the sun, which moves in and out behind the clouds and seems to smile at us, as if it's shining down on us with approval. Most kingdoms were probably taken by violent force, but ours is taken without a struggle, and we aren't putting anybody out of their home. We are simply taking what doesn't belong to anybody else, and hadn't even existed before.

SAMI: "Let's hang the flag."

ME: "Okay."

I select a spot close to the centre of the island and dig a hole. Sami pulls the flag out of his pack and ties it to the top of the pole. We sink one end of the pole into the hole, push it up straight, and stand back and stare at the flag.

CHARLIE: "It's pink."

SAMI: "Yeah."

CHARLIE: "How come it's pink?"

SAMI: "Pink is the best colour to let everyone know that they are welcome. It's the colour of tolerance, and . . . it was the only decent material I could find."

ME: "I like it. But what's *on* it? We can't see it because there's no wind."

SAMI: "It's a sprouted seed. I sewed it on."

ME: "A sprouted seed?"

SAMI: "Yeah."

ME: "That's good, I guess."

SAMI: "It's a symbol for growth."

CHARLIE: "I saw it; it looks like a turd."

SAMI: "It doesn't look like a turd."

CHARLIE: "It does. It looks like a purple turd with green hair and a pink background."

We all stare as the flagpole begins to lean. It leans slowly to one side, then picks up speed, and then smacks flat onto the ground.

SAMI: "You insulted our flag, Charlie."

CHARLIE: "I didn't insult it."

SAMI: "You have to treat it with respect, Charlie."

Sami looks at me. I nod my head.

ME: "You have to treat it with respect, Charlie."

CHARLIE: "I didn't mean any disrespect. Let's straighten it up."

ME: "Okay."

SAMI: "Where'd you get this flagpole anyway, Billy? It doesn't stay up very well."

ME: "It's an old clothesline pole. We just need to dig a deeper hole."

We try three more times, but the flagpole won't stay up in the sandy soil.

SAMI: "There's an old flagpole in the woods behind the school, a real flagpole. Why don't we take it and set it up here properly? I don't want our flag to hang from a clothesline pole."

CHARLIE: "I don't want a clothesline pole."

ME: "Okay. Let's get it tomorrow and carry it over. That'd be cool: a real flagpole."

CHARLIE: "I want a real flagpole."

ME: "Okay."

CHARLIE: "Let's sing our anthem."

SAMI: "Let's wait till the flag is flying. We should sing the anthem when we can see the flag."

ME: "Agreed."

CHARLIE: "Okay."

ME: "We should put the name of our country on a sign and hammer it into the ground, too, so people will know what it is."

SAMI: "Yeah."

CHARLIE: "Okay."

ME: "My mom's got a whole bunch of wooden letters in the garage. I could probably find enough to spell the name of our country. We could nail them onto a board and paint them."

SAMI: "Sounds good."

CHARLIE: "Sounds good."

ME: "Excellent."

The next morning, we meet in the field behind the school. At the back of the field is a woods, with a ditch that's always dry except during heavy rains. In the ditch is the old flagpole. We have all seen it before. It looks a lot bigger once we stare at it with the intention of carrying it to the river. When we try to lift it, we're in for a shock. It weighs a ton.

CHARLIE: "This is impossible."

SAMI: "But it's perfect. Everybody will see our flag for miles. We have to have it. Come on, let's carry it."

ME: "Sami, we can't carry it. It's too heavy."

CHARLIE: "We'll all get hernias."

ME: "What's a hernia?"

CHARLIE: "I don't know, but it's from lifting something too heavy, and it's really bad."

SAMI: "Let's just try."

ME: "It's impossible, Sami."

CHARLIE: "I don't want to get a hernia."

ME: "Just a minute you guys."

I look around. Some players from the basketball team are practising in the courtyard behind the school. They're older than us. I recognize Jason Knight, who's in my sister's class, and who really likes her. I don't know why. He's an athlete; she's a scholar. She thinks that athletes are born with hairy armpits. But as I watch them jump up and down on the court, I get an idea. Maybe it's not the smartest idea in the world, but it's an idea.

ME: "Let's ask those guys to carry our flagpole down to the river."

CHARLIE: "Why would they do that for us?"

ME: "I don't know, I'll make a deal."

CHARLIE: "What deal?"

ME: "I don't know. I'll figure something out."

SAMI: "What deal?"

ME: "Just wait."

I run across the field, push open the gate, and enter the court where they are playing basketball. Our quest fills me with a boldness I have never felt before.

"Hey Jason!"

They stop jumping. The ball rolls into the fence. Everyone turns and looks at me.

"What?"

"Could you guys give us a hand with a flagpole?"

"What?"

"We have to carry a flagpole down to the river and we need help. It's too heavy."

"No way. Carry it yourself."

They pick up the ball and continue the game.

"We can't. It's too heavy."

They ignore me. One of them bumps into me and knocks me down by accident. I pick myself up and keep trying.

"It's not that far."

"No way."

"It's good exercise. It'll make you stronger."

"You're in the way."

And then, I say it. I don't plan it; don't think it through, like whether or not it is a good idea. I just say it.

"My sister will go out with you if you do."

The ball stops again and rolls into the fence. Nobody says anything. Jason comes over and stands in front of me. He's all sweaty and his muscles are bulging inside his shirt. I wonder if I will ever have muscles like that.

"She will?"

"Yes."

"Are you sure?"

"Yes."

"Okay, show us the pole."

They follow me back to the ditch, Jason and four others, where Sami and Charlie are standing around like gremlins who just wandered out of the woods. They look so much smaller all of a sudden. Jason stares at the pole, looks in the direction of the river, and says, "Okay, let's do this."

They grab the pole, pull it out of the ditch as if it's made of cardboard, and start off at a trot. Sami, Charlie, and I hold on as well, so as to look like we are helping, but we are probably just slowing them down. A few times on the way to the river I catch a glimpse of Sami's eyes and I know exactly what he's thinking: these guys would make an awesome army for our kingdom.

It takes only minutes to get to the river, and a few more for them to carry the flagpole through the water and drop it onto the ground. Then Jason comes close to me and looks me in the eye. He's a nice guy. Why wouldn't my sister want to go out with him?

"Tell her I'll call her tonight."

"Okay."

They swim back across the river, run up the bank, and disappear. We watch them go. They look like young lions in the sun.

SAMI: "What deal did you make?"

ME: "I don't know. Nothing."

CHARLIE: "What did you say?"

ME: "Nothing."

CHARLIE: "You had to say *something*. Those guys wouldn't carry our pole all the way here for nothing. What did you say?"

SAMI: "What was the deal, Billy? We have a right to know. Tell us."

ME: "Okay. I told Jason that Merilee would go out with him."

Sami and Charlie stare at me with shocked faces.

ME: "What? What's the big deal? She won't go out with him. He'll ask her, and she'll simply say no. What's the big deal?"

SAMI: "You're toast."

ME: "No."

SAMI: "You are so toast, and you don't even know it."

ME: "What's the big deal? He's just going to call her."

CHARLIE: "You can stay at my place tonight if you need to."

ME: "Why are you guys making such a big deal out of this? It's fine. My sister won't mind. She'll understand when I explain it to her. You guys are acting like it's my funeral or something."

# Chapter 6

IN THE MIDDLE of the night I feel someone enter my room. I wake up and Merilee is standing over my bed.

"You little shite! You sold me out!"

"What? What's that smell? Something smells really bad."

"It's dog poo."

I raise my head and see Merilee holding a plastic bag in one hand. She's wearing rubber gloves.

"What are you doing with dog poo?" I'm afraid to know.

"I'm going to smear it on you."

"No! Please! Don't do it!"

"You sold me out, you little worm. I'm going to shove this dog poo so far up your nose you're going to smell dogs' bottoms for the rest of your life and you're going to like it."

"No! Please! Don't do it! Have mercy!"

There is an awkward silence while she stands over me. My mind is racing. Merilee is thinking.

"Don't do it. I'll do anything."

"Hmmm. Bearing in mind that this will likely traumatize you for life, I am willing to commute your sentence on one condition."

"What? Anything! Anything! I'll do it."

"Your allowance for the summer. It's mine."

"My allowance?" I try to imagine the summer without candy, pop, or any new video games. I wonder how much I can borrow from Sami and Charlie.

"Your allowance. Hurry up and decide. This bag is getting slippery."

"For the whole summer?"

"From right now till school starts. Hurry up!"

"Uhh . . . okay!"

"You agree?"

"Yes."

"Then say it. Say, 'My allowance is yours until the first day of school.'"

"My allowance is yours till the first day of school."

"And, 'I will never *ever* sell out my sister again, so long as I live.'"

"I will never ever sell out my sister again."

"So long as I live."

"So long as I live."

"Okay. Done. And you'd better remember this or everybody's going to call you the boy who stinks of dog poo."

"I'll remember."

"You'd better. Little worm. I can't believe you sold me out."

"I'm sorry."

Merilee leaves the room and I pull the blankets tighter around me. I can still smell dog poo, and even after ten minutes I can still smell it, so I get up, turn on the light, and look under the bed. There isn't anything there, but I'm sure I can smell it, and I can still smell it when I wake up in the morning.

We bring two more shovels to the kingdom and take turns digging a deeper hole. Beneath the sandy soil the ground is rocky, and it is a lot of hard work. It's hot out, and we have to stop often to drink water and eat the peanut butter and jam sandwiches we made at my house. My mom was glad we were going on a hike, which was what I told her, and what Charlie told his parents, but Sami didn't have to tell anyone because there was no one home.

Once the hole is deep enough, we shove the big end of the pole into it, then tie a long rope to the top end, and the three of us lean back like in a tug-of-war, and pull with all our strength until the pole stands up more or less straight. It isn't perfectly straight but it is close enough. Then we fill in the rest of the hole with rocks and sand and pack it down hard by jumping on it.

Now the pole doesn't seem so big because the thickest part is in the ground. Sami ties on the flag and pulls it up close to the top with a smaller rope that runs through a pulley. Once the flag is up, a small wind blows it open. It's awesome! It's pink with a purple seed and green blades sticking out the top. It looks like a pineapple to me. It is a happy flag.

Then we sing the anthem. Charlie made copies of the words, and he dances while Sami and I sing. It is another important moment for us, even though Sami and I keep mixing up the words.

Then we have lunch. While we sit on the ground and eat sandwiches and drink chocolate milk, we watch a canoe come down the river. The people inside are taking pictures, and the canoe keeps winding back and forth from one bank to the other.

CHARLIE: "Do you think they'll stop here?"

ME: "I doubt it."

SAMI: "They might."

CHARLIE: "We should charge them a toll."

ME: "What? Are you serious?"

CHARLIE: "Dead serious. This is our country. If they want to dock and get out, they should pay a toll."

I look at Sami.

SAMI: "Yeah, they should probably pay a toll."

ME: "But they don't even know it's a country. We don't have our sign up yet."

SAMI: "Quick! Let's put up our sign."

CHARLIE: "Yeah!"

ME: "Okay, but I don't think we should charge them a toll."

I pull the wooden letters out of my pack. We nailed wires to them that were made for sticking into the ground. I pull out a hammer and start hammering them into the rocky sand at the top end of the island, where the canoe will probably dock, if they dock. We have just enough letters to spell KINGDOM OF NO WORRIES, all in capitals. I'm still hammering the last letters in when the canoe stops gently at the water's edge.

LADY: "Hello there!"

Her friend doesn't say anything.

ME: "Hi."

CHARLIE: "This is private property. You have to pay a toll if you want to get out of the canoe."

LADY: "Private property? Are you sure?"

She smiles but looks confused.

SAMI: "It's a new country. It's called the Kingdom of No Worries."

He points to the flagpole.

SAMI: "That's our flag."

She smiles even more. She is very friendly.

LADY: "I like your flag. And I love the name of your country. How much is the toll?"

CHARLIE: "What?"

We haven't decided how much it will be yet.

SAMI: "For a canoe it's two dollars."

The lady turns around and looks at her friend who's sitting in the back of the canoe and isn't smiling.

LADY: "Have you got two dollars?"

He reaches into his pocket, finds a coin, and tosses it towards Charlie. Charlie picks it up like it's a piece of gold and puts it in his pocket.

CHARLIE: "I'll put it in our bank."

We look at each other because we know that we don't have a bank yet and will have to make one.

SAMI: "Okay, you can come and stay now."

LADY: "Great! Can I take pictures?"

She steps out of the canoe. She's wearing a camera around her neck.

Charlie looks at me, and I know he's thinking we should charge her for taking pictures, but I shake my head because that's too much.

ME: "Sure. Take all you like."

LADY: "Can I take pictures of the three of you, standing in your new country?"

We grin at each other.

ME: "Sure. Why not?"

So we stand together in front of our country name, and we stand in front of the flag. We stand with our arms crossed and try to look important, and we stand with our hands in our pockets and smile. The lady takes a lot of pictures. She asks us our names and a whole bunch of questions about our country, and then she thanks us and gets back in her canoe and leaves. We think that is it and we'll never see her again. But that's when it all begins.

# Chapter 7

THE NEXT MORNING, we wake up to find ourselves on the front page of the newspaper.

Dad brings it into the house. "Hey, look at these kids down on the river. They claim to have started their own country. Isn't that a hoot? Hey, look, Billy. These kids look just like you and your friends. Look, Ella, these kids look just like . . ." Dad pauses. "Oh my Lord!" Then he turns and stares at me as if I am an alien that has come from another planet and has been living undercover with our family all these years. "That's you, Billy, isn't it?" He holds up the paper.

I stare at it. The picture isn't one of the ones we had posed for. Instead, it shows Sami gazing into the camera with a concentrated, kind of sad look on his face. Charlie is staring in one direction, and I'm staring in the other. We look like we are just waiting for something to happen. But Sami's expression steals the show. He looks deeply thoughtful. Probably he was just trying to decide what to eat next, but it looks a lot more important than that. The headline at the top of the article says, RIVER KINGDOM OFFERS HOPE FOR BETTER WORLD.

"Billy, that's you!" says Dad.

"I never knew that lady would put our picture in the paper."

Dad sits down and reads the article. Mom stands behind him and reads it, too. She steals little glances at me while she does. I think she's also trying to decide if I'm an alien. Then Dad holds up the paper and reads some of it out loud.

*"Everyone is welcome,"* say the boys. *"We want our country to be a model of tolerance and freedom for the whole world."*

Mom is beaming now. "Billy, that is wonderful. I am so proud of you."

"Thanks, Mom."

Merilee comes into the kitchen. Any time Mom or Dad say they are proud of me, Merilee can hear it from far away and will come to investigate. Usually she'll find reasons not to be proud of me, but this time she takes a look at the paper, takes a look at me, and then doesn't say anything.

"Look, Merki," says Dad. "Your little brother made the news."

Merilee takes the paper from Dad and reads the article lightning fast, then passes it back. "Hmmm."

That can mean anything from "that's crazy!" to "that's amazing!" Probably it's somewhere in between.

By late morning we're back in our country. It's sunny but cool for the end of June. Since our clothes are all wet from crossing the river, we are cold. We decide it will be a good idea to try to find a rubber dinghy, or maybe make a raft for crossing back and forth between Canada and the kingdom, or bring spare clothes. We have to run around the island to warm up. We notice a small group of people on one bank of the river watching us.

CHARLIE: "What do you think they want?"

ME: "Nothing. They're just curious."

SAMI: "We're kind of famous now."

ME: "I wonder if anyone will try to come over."

SAMI: "What would we do?"

ME: "I don't know."

CHARLIE: "Charge them a toll."

ME: "No way. We can't keep charging people money, Charlie. We'll get a reputation for being greedy. We don't want people to think that our kingdom is a greedy place."

SAMI: "Definitely not."

CHARLIE: "I don't see what's wrong with charging money. Seems to me like a good way to get rich."

ME: "But our country is not about getting rich, Charlie, it's more than that."

SAMI: "It's way more than that."

CHARLIE: "I don't see anything wrong with getting rich while we're at it. We could be millionaires before we're twenty, and then we wouldn't even have to work. We could just collect money from tolls and taxes."

SAMI: "What's that lady doing?"

ME: "What lady?"

I turn and watch as an old, white-haired lady steps into the river carrying something in her hands. She seems to know the shallowest place to cross, and she doesn't stop when the river comes up past her belly. She walks slowly across the river and comes to the edge of our land, where she stops and waits for us to meet her, which we do. She has a strange expression on her face. It's a smile and a serious look at the same time. She looks kind of sad, yet very determined. She holds up the thing in her hands and we see that it is a plant with tiny red flowers on it. She holds it out.

LADY: "A gift for the Kingdom of No Worries. Please accept my gift."

I step into the water and take the plant. The lady looks very pleased when I do.

LADY: "Dig a little hole for it, and don't overwater it. God bless you, boys."

Then she turns around and walks back across the river. She never actually steps onto our land, so Charlie can't ask her for a toll.

ME: "Thank you!"

I call it out after her, but she is concentrating on where to place her feet and never turns around. I carry the plant back to Sami and Charlie.

SAMI: "What are we going to do with that?"

CHARLIE: "Sell it."

ME: "No, we're going to plant it. This is the beginning of our garden."

SAMI: "Awesome."

I pick up the shovel and dig a hole. We pull the plant out of its pot and place it in the ground. Then we step back and stare at it.

SAMI: "It's growing here now."

Charlie and I nod our heads.

CHARLIE: "Yeah, it's awesome."

During the afternoon, three more people cross the river with plants. By suppertime we have dug seven holes and planted seven plants in the ground. Some of the people come out of the water and step into the kingdom but we never charge anyone a toll. Just before dark, when the sun is low on the horizon, and the light on the island makes a golden glow, which is when the kingdom looks its best, the lady in the canoe returns and takes more pictures. This time she tells us her name: Elizabeth. And this time she takes pictures of the plants and flowers.

The next day there is an explosion of people crossing the river with plants in their arms, and we spend the whole day digging holes in the ground and giving the plants a new home. It is a warm day, and people are crossing the river in shorts, t-shirts, and bathing suits. There are people on the bank with cameras and cell-phones, too. There always seem to be at least one or two people, and sometimes a small group of people, and sometimes a small crowd. But in the evening, when Elizabeth comes down in her canoe, and is all by herself this time, there is another boat—a motorized rubber dinghy—and there are two police officers in it.

# Chapter 8

ELIZABETH KNOWS THAT the officers are coming, because she arrives just before them, hops out of her canoe, and takes pictures of them as they step into the kingdom. She makes the police a little nervous, I think, but she doesn't care. She waves hello to us first, and then starts clicking away.

The police officers look around first, as if they aren't even interested in us. They stare at our garden, and one of them takes a pad out of her pocket and writes something down. Then she looks up at our flag and writes something else. Finally, she and her partner come over. I'm feeling nervous. Charlie isn't.

CHARLIE: "This is our country. You have to pay a toll for docking your boat. It's two dollars."

I can't believe he has the nerve to say that. The police officers look at each other and smile.

OFFICER: "It's getting dark soon, boys. You'd better be getting home."

ME: "We will, officer."

OFFICER: "Boys. This is city property. You can't just plant what you like here. You have to get a permit."

I hear Elizabeth's camera clicking and see her write something down. One of the officers takes out another pad and starts writing on it. He asks us our names, ages, addresses, and phone numbers. Then he tears a paper from another pad. It's a ticket!

OFFICER: "You'll have to remove that flagpole tomorrow, boys, and all those plants. You must apply to the city for a permit before you can plant anything here. Do you understand?"

He steps forward and hands me the ticket.

OFFICER: "What you've done here is a violation of city property. This is just a warning. The next time it'll be a fine."

SAMI: "*This is our country.*"

Sami looks upset. The two officers just stand and stare for a while. I can tell that they aren't sure what to do.

OFFICER: "Remove these plants by tomorrow or face a fine. Take your skateboards to the park, boys, or go play baseball, but leave city property alone."

Then they get into their boat and motor away.

I feel crushed.

All night I toss and turn. In the morning I meet Merilee in the kitchen and tell her what happened.

"I don't think they can make you take the flagpole down or dig up the plants."

"Really?"

"No, I don't think so, because they don't have the right to force you to do something. That would be oppression. What they can do is prevent you from doing any more of something that is unlawful, which is what you're doing in their minds. And probably it is. Certainly the city will assume the island is its property, which means that it belongs to all of us, which means that the police force, who represent all of us, and are here to protect us, have the right to kick you off, and in so doing, protect you from yourself."

"That sounds crazy."

"I know, but it isn't if you think it through."

"Isn't there anything we can do? I don't want to go to jail."

"Pretty unlikely you'll go to jail. I suppose they could put you in a correctional institution though, if you misbehave enough."

"That's the same thing to me. Can't we do *anything*?"

"Hmmm . . . it's conceivable that if you confront the police with an act of civil disobedience, which raises enough support from local citizens to put political pressure on the city, which controls the police force, then you could potentially make the police stand down. But that's a long shot. I mean, it happens, but it's rare."

"What's civil disobedience?"

"Organized defiance with a political agenda."

"Which means . . ?"

"I've got an essay about it by Henry David Thoreau. It's upstairs. It will tell you all about it."

"That's okay. Dad works for the city. Do you think he can help us?"

"I doubt it. More likely he'll just get caught in the middle."

I watch Merilee eat her cereal. There's such a sense of

purpose in everything she does. But the food she eats is fuel to keep her going, nothing else. I wonder if it ever occurs to her that eating can be fun.

"Can I ask you something?"

She takes a bite and answers with a full mouth.

"What?"

"How come you know so much?"

She gives me her long beak stare, which now looks like a pelican that has just swallowed a fish.

"I read."


Dad's out in the garage. He's reading the paper, and we are in it again. He has a kind of sad look on his face. I'm waiting for him to tell me to get down to the river quick and tear up those plants and pull down the flagpole. Dad doesn't like confrontation. He prefers to get along with everybody, which sometimes just means getting out of their way.

But that's not what he says. What he says makes me feel ten feet tall. And he speaks to me in a way he never has before.

"You made the paper again, Billy."

I go over and take a look. The picture shows the two police officers talking to us, and once again Sami's face is in the front, and it is upset and a little angry. The police are towering over us, pointing to the plants. The headline reads, KINGDOM OF NO WORRIES ORDERED OUT!

Dad's expression is a little angry, too. I'm surprised. But it's the words he says next that really surprise me, and they stay in my mind all day.

"Keep your head up today, Billy. Looks like you're in for a rough ride."

"Thanks, Dad." My spine tingles as I step out of the garage.

It turns out that Dad isn't the only one who's upset by the newspaper. When I meet Sami and Charlie, and we cross the river, we see a small crowd on the other riverbank. They are carrying more plants than the day before, and some are carrying posters that say, "Save the Kingdom of No Worries."

Wow.

People cross the river to bring us their plants, but it isn't long before two more police officers show up, though they don't come in a boat, and don't come to the kingdom. They stand on the riverbank and speak through a megaphone.

"You are in violation of city property. Remove those

plants and take down that flagpole. I repeat: remove those plants and take down that flagpole."

Now I'm really nervous. I don't want to get arrested. I remember Merilee saying that they can't *make* us do things; they can only *prevent* us from doing things. Suddenly some of the people who brought plants pick up our shovels and start planting. The police stand by and watch. Now they won't have to arrest just us; they'll have to arrest a whole bunch of people, which they don't look ready to do.

Soon even more people come, and some are carrying drums and folding chairs. They approach us, shake our hands, tell us their names, which we can't remember, and say that they are drummers from Senegal. Would we mind if they performed in our kingdom? We say that would be great. In a few moments we hear hands slapping on drums, which is a sound that makes you want to get up and dance.

And so, while the police watch from the riverbank, people start dancing to the music of drums, and a wonderful energy fills the kingdom.

# Chapter 9

THE DRUMMERS FROM Senegal are still drumming when Sami, Charlie, and I go home. It is way past our bedtime, but Mom and Dad know where I am, and Charlie's parents know where he is, and Sami's parents don't care.

I climb into bed with the beating of drums still echoing inside my head. It was so nice when the moon came out and the silhouettes of a hundred people were standing around, or sitting, or gently dancing to the music. We had no idea our kingdom would become so popular.

Elizabeth showed up, too, and took photos and films of everything, and interviewed the drummers.

In the morning we make the front page once again. Well, Sami, Charlie, and I don't, but the kingdom does. There is a picture of the drummers and people waving their hands in the air. The headline reads, SENEGALESE DRUMMERS ROCK THE KINGDOM.

Before Merilee leaves for school, she glances at the paper, and then asks me a question. I know she is going to ask it before she does. Sometimes I can read her mind; I just can't always understand it.

"Have you read *The Republic* yet, Billyboy?"

"No, but I'm going to. I just didn't get a chance to yet."

"But you've been carrying it around in your pack like twenty-four-seven. Why don't you take it out and read it?"

"I know. I will. I've just been very busy lately."

She gives me her best bird-swallow-the-fish look. It gives me chills. It's actually really scary if you dare to imagine you are a fish.

"You can't run a country if you don't understand its politics. Someone will take it all away from you and you won't even know what happened. You have to read, Billyboy. Haven't you ever heard that knowledge is power?"

"Yes, but . . ."

"I have to go." She grabs a banana, looks into my eyes, and says one of the nicest things she's ever said to me. "In spite of our differences, you are my little brother. I'd hate to see them take it from you just because you're wandering around in a fog. There's a reason why they say the pen is mightier than the sword. Why don't you do yourself a favour and read the book?" Then she taps me on the shoulder and goes out the door.

I leave the house with *The Republic* in my pack and a tingle in my spine.

It's a great day. The sun is shining, birds are singing, and the summer is still just beginning. The music of drums is still in my head, though it is quieter now. I wonder how many people will come to the kingdom today. Our garden is amazing. There are plants of all sizes and shapes, and many colourful flowers. People take such care in planting them and watering them and talking to them, because a lot of people talk to their plants as if they were leaving them in a nursery school for the day.

But when I come down the street, cross the river road, and step onto the bank, I get a terrible shock. Our flag-pole has been knocked down. The garden has been dug up, and all the beautiful plants have been thrown onto a heap. A wooden sign stuck in the ground says, "No Trespassing!"

I look around. There are no police in sight. I feel like I've been kicked in the gut. It is so upsetting. My mind races, and I try to think of the things that Merilee said. Knowledge is power. The pen is mightier than the sword. Maybe, but it's hard to believe we can save our kingdom just by reading a book.

A little while later Charlie and Sami show up. They are even more upset than I am, and more angry.

SAMI: "We're going to fight."

CHARLIE: "We're going to kick their butts all over town."

ME: "How? We can't do anything."

CHARLIE: "Yes, we can. We're going back over there and are going to start all over again."

SAMI: "That's right!"

ME: "No! Wait, guys. We can't do that. They'll put us in jail."

SAMI: "Then let them put us in jail."

CHARLIE: "I want to go to jail."

ME: "No, you don't."

CHARLIE: "Yes, I do. I want to go to jail so that everybody can see the injustice that is being done."

SAMI: "I agree. Let's all go to jail."

CHARLIE: "And we can go on a hunger strike."

ME: "Are you crazy? I don't want to go on a hunger strike. And I don't want to go to jail. If we go to jail, we might never get out."

CHARLIE: "We have to fight for our country, Billie-Jean."

SAMI: "We have to fight, Billy."

ME: "Wait, guys, just wait! Let's think about it. We don't even know for sure that it was the police who did this."

SAMI: "Of course it was. Who else could it be?"

ME: "I don't know, I'm just saying that we never saw them do it, so we can't know for sure."

SAMI: "I think we know for sure."

CHARLIE: "Hey, look!"

We turn our heads and see a dozen or so people step into the kingdom from the other side of the river. They are carrying plants and chairs. They wave to us, and then they kick down the no-trespassing sign and start straightening up the flagpole.

SAMI: "Come on! Let's get over there!"

So Charlie climbs on top of Sami's back, and we rush

across the river as fast as we can. We receive a warm welcome from the people there. Some have been here before, and some are new. More keep coming! Everyone is so angry that the kingdom has been vandalized and police are trying to keep people out. I'm still nervous that we are breaking the law, but it's hard not to get carried away with the energy and enthusiasm all around us.

By noon, the garden is replanted, bigger than before, the flagpole is up, straighter than before, and there are hundreds of people with chairs, umbrellas, coolers, guitars, Frisbees, and hula-hoops. The Senegalese drummers return in the evening, and by then there are probably a thousand people on our island kingdom.

We see a dozen people carrying over two heavy plastic boxes, which turn out to be portable toilets. That's great, because people were peeing in the river, or crossing to use bathrooms in fast food restaurants, which was really inconvenient.

In the early twilight Elizabeth comes by, and this time she brings along a whole film crew, including the host of a local news show. She says they want to interview us for television. Would we mind?

So we clear a space and set up three chairs in front of the garden. While the drummers drum softly in the background, we take turns answering the host's questions. I'm surprised by how well we answer. You'd think we had prepared for it.

HOST: "So what gave you boys the idea to start your own country?"

SAMI: "We wanted to create a place that was a model of tolerance for the world."

HOST: "That's very inspiring. What do you mean by tolerance? Who will you allow to enter your country?"

ME: "Everyone, except people who are planning to hurt other people, like neo-Nazis, and haters, and terrorists."

HOST: "Does this mean then that you will permit people who hold different political views from yours?"

SAMI & ME: "Yes."

HOST: "And different religious views?"

CHARLIE: "Yes. All religions and genders are welcome."

HOST: "That sounds wonderful. You call your country a kingdom. Is it really a monarchy then? Do you have a king?"

CHARLIE: "It's a democracy. We just like the name of kingdom."

ME: "It's a constitutional monarchy. Everyone has a vote."

HOST: "So it's equal?"

SAMI & CHARLIE & ME: "Yes."

HOST: "This morning you found your garden torn up, your flagpole knocked down, and no-trespassing signs posted. How do you respond to that?"

ME: "We do not wish to break the law, we just want our country recognized."

HOST: "I see. And to what extent are you willing to go to have your country recognized?"

SAMI: "We are willing to go to jail."

CHARLIE: "If we are put in jail, we will go on a hunger strike."

HOST: "Amazing. How old are you boys?"

CHARLIE & ME: "Twelve."

SAMI: "I'm turning thirteen."

HOST: "And you're willing to go to jail?"

SAMI & CHARLIE: "Yes."

HOST: "As I look around me I see what must be a thousand people here, all enjoying themselves. This island kingdom has become some sort of retreat right in the heart of our city. How do you boys feel about that? Are you pleased that you have created a place where people can come to escape the stress of their daily lives?"

SAMI & CHARLIE & ME: "Yes. We love that."

HOST: "Where do you see all this going?"

We look at each other. We don't know.

ME: "Utopia."

I don't know what that means exactly, but I know it's supposed to be a good place. I'll have to ask Merilee when I get home.

# Chapter 10

LONG AFTER WE GO home and climb into bed, the music, laughter, and dancing continue on in the kingdom, and enough people stay right through the night to prevent anyone from tearing up the garden again or knocking down the flagpole. When we arrive the next morning, we expect to find the police there, but we don't. Instead, we are greeted by a handful of weary-eyed partygoers who are just now on their way home to bed. The kingdom is filled with chairs, coolers left behind, the two portable toilets, and a whole bunch of umbrellas stuck in the sandy soil or folded and lying on their side. Sami, Charlie, and I walk around and fold the umbrellas so they won't blow away, and we pick up garbage and tidy the chairs. But we leave a few umbrellas up because it's nice to have shade from the sun. We still expect to see the police, but they don't show up. By noon, we start receiving visitors of a different sort.

The first is a man in a dark suit. He walks down to the riverbank and waves to us from there. He's carrying a sign and a bag in his hand. He keeps waving and hoping we'll cross the river to talk to him, but Sami says we should stay here and let him come to us. Charlie agrees with that so I agree, too, though I'm certain the man will never enter the river in his suit.

I'm wrong. Once he realizes we aren't coming over, he takes off his shoes, socks, and jacket, rolls up his pants, rolls his socks neatly into his shoes, and steps carefully into the water. Holding the sign and bag above his head, he crosses the river in his bare feet. We all stare, bewildered, wondering what he wants.

Judging from his sign, he's from the Bank of Ontario, which we can see from our seats in the shade of an umbrella. Stepping out of the water, he comes over with a friendly but a kind of forced smile.

BANKER: "Hi boys!"

SAMI & ME: "Hi."

BANKER: "Nice day, hey?"

ME: "Not too bad."

BANKER: "This is a terrific experiment you've got going here, boys. Very interesting to see."

CHARLIE: "What do you want?"

The bank manager smiles.

BANKER: "I can see that you boys have a strong sense of what's what, so I won't beat around the bush. I'm from the Bank of Ontario."

He points to his building.

BANKER: "As we have noticed, you boys are receiving quite a bit of attention for this experiment you've got going here . . ."

CHARLIE: "It's not an experiment; it's a country."

BANKER: "My apologies, your country. As you are receiving quite a bit of attention, we at our bank are wondering if we can make a deal with you."

SAMI: "What kind of deal?"

BANKER: "We are willing to offer you boys a small sum of money if you would allow us to place our sign on this island in a strategically visible spot."

CHARLIE: "How much money?"

BANKER: "Two hundred dollars."

We don't know what to do. I can tell that Charlie really wants the money. Well, we all want it. Sami doesn't need it like Charlie and I do. I don't have any allowance anymore, though I've been too busy lately to notice. But the main problem is that we don't know how it will look to have the bank's sign on the ground. I know this is what we are all thinking, even though we never have a chance to discuss it first.

BANKER: "It's just a small advertisement, boys. You'll hardly see it."

CHARLIE: "I don't see any problem with that."

Charlie looks at Sami and me.

ME: "I don't care, I guess."

Sami never says anything, but sort of nods his head.

CHARLIE: "But it will cost you three hundred dollars."

The bank manager never blinks.

BANKER: "Three hundred dollars it is."

He takes an envelope out of the plastic bag. It has several hundred-dollar bills inside. I wonder how high he would have gone. He hands us each a hundred-dollar bill, then pulls a hammer out of the bag, walks over to a spot in front of the flagpole, and hammers the sign into the ground. It is a golden sign and it looks kind of nice there.

By suppertime, there are four more signs in front of

the flagpole: two from insurance companies, one from another bank, and one for a hospital fund. We don't charge the hospital but charge the insurance companies the same as the banks. Nobody blinks at the cost. Suddenly, we have twelve hundred dollars, well, twelve hundred and two.

And that isn't the only deal we make that day. A pizza deliveryman from Green Daddy's Pizza, the best pizza in Briffin, crosses the river with three extra-large pizzas on his head. They're freebies, and he tells us we can have free pizza every day of the summer if we hang a Green Daddy's Pizza banner on one of the portable toilets. We agree immediately.

A little while later, we're sitting in our chairs, watching the sun go down, eating pizza, listening to drums, and discussing what to do with our money, when two ladies cross the river with cardboard boxes above their heads. They have unhappy expressions on their faces. We watch them come out of the water and walk straight to us, even though there are lots of other people around. Everyone knows us from the newspapers.

The two ladies put the boxes down in front of us, stand up, and wipe the sweat from their faces. Their clothes are all wet now and cling tightly to their bodies, which doesn't look very good. The people who come to the island and stay usually carry extra clothes, and change in the portable toilets. Even though it's warm out, the wind can make you cold if you are soaking wet.

One of the ladies does all the talking. The other one looks too shy.

LADY: "Hello there."

SAMI & CHARLIE & ME: "Hi."

LADY: "We have come here as a last resort. We have been all over the city, trying to find support to help us keep our shelter open."

ME: "Shelter?"

LADY: "Our animal shelter."

ME: "Oh."

LADY: "We run the Briffin Shelter for Wounded Puppies and Kittens, but the city has cut our funding in favour of the bigger, fancier shelters, even though most of them don't give as much attention to the younger wounded animals that are less likely to be adopted, and so the crippled little creatures usually end up on our doorstep. But if we don't keep up with an increase in our rent, we'll be out on the street by the end of the week. And so we're going all over the city to try to raise enough money to keep our shelter open, but . . ."

Both ladies look ready to cry.

LADY: "No one seems to care."

I look at Sami and Charlie. Sami has a "Why are these people bothering us?" look on his face, and Charlie has a "They can't have any of our money" look on his face. I'm not sure. Then the ladies open up the boxes and show us what is inside.

The first one holds a little kitten on a towel. It's stinky because the kitten has gone to the bathroom on the towel. The kitten is very small and weak, and when it looks up at us we see that it has only one eye. One of its ears has been chewed off, too.

LADY: "We found her in an alley. Someone threw her out, and she was attacked by a raccoon. She's still pretty weak, but she'll make it if we can find her a home."

My heart jumps into my throat. I look over at Charlie. His face is melting like ice cream on a hot stove. I've never seen him look like that before. I look at Sami. His face is turning into a baloney sandwich. He's upset. Then the lady opens up the other box, and we see a little puppy looking up at us with the saddest eyes. It is frightened to death and shaking, as if it thinks we are going to beat it. The lady picks him up, and then we see that he has only three legs. She passes him to Sami, who takes him and cuddles him in his arms as if he is the most precious thing in the world.

SAMI: "He has no place to live?"

His voice sounds broken.

LADY: "None. But we're looking after him."

CHARLIE: "But what if you can't pay your rent?"

LADY: "We'll find a way. We won't abandon them."

The warm wind comes gently up the river. The sound of drums and people laughing and dancing and having fun are all around us, but none of that seems to matter anymore.

ME: "How much money do you need to stay open?"

LADY: "Five thousand dollars."

She wipes the sweat from her face again.

LADY: "But we know the Lord will provide. We have collected some already."

CHARLIE: "How much?"

LADY: "Three hundred dollars."

She hands the kitten to Charlie, who can't take his eyes off it. Charlie holds the kitten close to his chest, and the kitten looks up at him sideways with its one eye, and Charlie looks down at it, and his eyes are full of water.

CHARLIE: "We can give you twelve hundred dollars."

I swallow hard. That's all of our money. I look over at

Sami. He's patting the puppy gently and nodding his head. The lady's mouth drops and her eyes open wide.

LADY: "Really? Really, boys? Can you help us that much?"

CHARLIE: "We want to help the animals."

SAMI: "That's what the Kingdom of No Worries is all about."

So we give the ladies the twelve hundred dollars the kingdom has earned this very day, and they carry the kitten and puppy back across the river. Then we sit down and finish our pizza. We feel like kings.

# Chapter 11

THE DAYS ARE LONG on the river. The sun and wind have a way of sucking the energy out of you like moisture from a flower, so that when I go home each night, I fall asleep instantly. Sometimes I don't even undress; I just collapse on my bed, planning to get up and brush my teeth in a minute, and then don't wake until the sun is up.

The night we give our money to the shelter I meet Merilee on my way upstairs. She has a strange look on her face, and I know she wants to talk. I'm afraid she'll try to keep me up, and I'm desperate to sleep, so I try to control the conversation and keep walking towards my room. But she stands in my way.

"How's school?" I say.

"Pretty good," she says. She looks funny. Now I'm wondering what's on her mind.

"What are you studying?" I hate even asking what somebody is studying in the summertime. It feels like a betrayal to life.

"Current events."

"Oh." I yawn as loudly as I can.

"We watch news clips from around the country. Then we write essays about them."

"Interesting." I try to get past her, but she blocks my way.

"Do you want to know what we watched today?"

Not really. "What?"

"You."

"*What*? Me?"

"Yeah. Isn't that a hoot? We watched an interview you and your buddies made for the current events channel. It was surprisingly good. You guys actually sounded like you knew what you were talking about."

"We were faking it. Are you really studying us in school?"

"Yes."

"That's weird."

"Isn't it?"

For a moment we don't speak. I'm wondering if I can ask for my allowance back. Probably not. She wouldn't give it back on principle. I can still smell dog poo in my room, unless it's just my imagination. Maybe she dropped a little bit on the floor. I should clean my room.

"Anyway . . . we have to come over and interview you."

"Really? You're coming to the kingdom to interview us?"

"We have to. It's part of our course. We could either interview *you*, or we could go to the golf course and interview the owners about reports they're using illegal fertilizers, but that's twelve kilometres away, and we'd have to take three buses to get there, and Mehra gets motion sickness on buses, so . . ."

"Oh."

"So we'll see you tomorrow, Billyboy."

"Okay."

By evening there are so many people in the kingdom there are almost no open spaces, except for the river's edge. Dogs run loose, splash in the water, and chase Frisbees, which is fun to watch. There are long line-ups for the toilets, but everyone is relaxed and friendly. No one seems to mind.

Tonight there are a lot of people who have come to the kingdom with some sort of request. They have to form a line to wait their turn to talk to us. It isn't our fault. We are happy to talk to everybody, but you can't talk to everybody at the same time. Besides, people want to talk in privacy, and the only way they can do that is if we sit together away from everybody else.

People have started calling us the Council. I guess that works. It's not *our* name but what people want to call us, and the name just sticks. So if you come to the kingdom and want something, you have to speak to the Council, which is us.

In the line-up tonight are a couple of guys with tents and sleeping bags. They're kind of dirty and smelly, but one of them has a really nice dog. We are official animal lovers now that we're supporting a local shelter for wounded puppies and kittens. We have decided that the kingdom should be a sanctuary for all animals.

When the two young men stand in front of us, they can't take their eyes away from our pizza.

ME: "Would you like some pizza?"

MAN: "Yeah. That'd be great."

They help themselves. They're starving. We give their dog a slice, too. We always have more pizza than we can eat because Green Daddy's brings over three extra-large pizzas and six cans of pop every night. After the Council eats theirs, somebody else always finishes the rest. For our part we make sure Green Daddy's banner hangs clearly from one of the toilets, where everybody can see it.

The two guys tell us they and their dog are homeless. We say we understand. Then they ask if they can pitch their tents in the kingdom and stay for a while. We look at each other and think about it.

SAMI: "We don't have that much room."

MAN: "There's a spot over there. We saw it. We can squeeze our tents close together, and we won't bother anybody. We promise. If anybody complains, we promise we'll leave."

He sounds kind of desperate. I shrug my shoulders. Sami does, too. Charlie looks like he doesn't care. He's only interested in their dog. He's not asking people for money anymore. Ever since we gave the shelter all our money, he's changed. I don't know how exactly; I can just feel it.

ME: "Yeah, I guess so."

MAN: "Oh, that's great!"

They both reach over and shake our hands. Their hands are greasy.

Next in line is an old man from the Briffin Bach Society. He explains that the Briffin Bach Society is trying to keep classical music alive in our community, and they want to know if they can come over on Sunday afternoon and sing.

We shrug again and say that that sounds okay, but warn that Sunday afternoon is pretty busy in the kingdom, and noisy, and they might have a hard time being heard.

OLD MAN: "Don't worry about that. We'll sing real loud."

Then he smiles, thanks us, and steps into the river. As I watch him go, I feel amazed by how many people are willing to get wet to come to the kingdom. It seems to bother them less than waiting in traffic.

Next in line is a company that sells grass. A middle-aged man, who looks a little like my dad, starts to tell us how great the island would look if it were covered with grass. For a very reasonable sum, we can have the entire kingdom covered with grass sods. Are we interested?

Firstly, we explain, we can't afford it. Secondly, even if we could afford it, the grass would get trampled immediately by all the people here. Look around, I say. The man looks around at all the people, sighs, and shrugs his shoulders. Then he steps into the river. I look at Charlie and Sami and they roll their eyes.

CHARLIE: "He just wanted our money."

ME: "We don't have any money, Charlie."

The next person tells us she has been on the island all day but forgot to bring a lunch. She wonders if there is any pizza left. Sami opens one of the boxes and gives her the last two slices.

WOMAN: "Any pop?"

ME: "Sorry, it's all gone."

WOMAN: "That's okay. I'll just drink from the river."

When she steps out of the way, we're staring into the faces of the Three Fates.

# Chapter 12

WORDS CANNOT DESCRIBE how weird it is. Sami, Charlie, and I sit in a semi-circle in our lawn chairs, forming the Council of the Kingdom of No Worries, the ultimate authority on the island, while Merilee, Mehra, and Marcie stand humbly in front of us. Maybe *humble* is not the best word to describe them.

MERILEE: "Finally!"

ME: "Sorry. We've been busy."

MERILEE: "Well, if your elevated highnesses wouldn't mind stooping so low, would you be willing to answer a few questions?"

SAMI: "Sure."

CHARLIE: "Shoot."

MERILEE: "Why do you call this nascent country a kingdom? Aren't kingdoms outdated and irrelevant today?"

SAMI: "Not at all. Our kingdom, like the Kingdom of Lesotho, is a constitutional monarchy. It's very relevant today. Look around."

Sami gestures for the Fates to look at all the people, which they do.

CHARLIE: "We like the name."

MEHRA: "We notice you have advertisements from banks, insurance companies, and pizzerias. Are you creating revenue?"

Mehra is exactly the same height as Merilee, and they look like sisters, except that Mehra is from India, and her hair is a little darker and her skin a little more tanned. Sometimes she wears a sari, and then so does Merilee and Marcie, so they all look like they're from India.

CHARLIE: "What's revenue?"

MERILEE: "Money."

ME: "Yes."

MARCIE: "Very much money?"

Marcie is a little shorter than Merilee and Mehra but can pass for their sister, too.

SAMI: "Yes."

Marcie's eyes open wide.

MARCIE: "Then you are obviously pursuing a capitalist economy."

CHARLIE: "We gave it away."

MERILEE: "You gave it away?"

She looks horrified at the thought that we gave our money away.

MERILEE: "To whom?"

ME: "The Briffin Shelter for Wounded Puppies and Kittens."

MEHRA: "How much money did you give them?"

SAMI: "That's a state secret."

CHARLIE: "Twelve hundred dollars."

MERILEE: "Twelve hundred dollars! You gave away twelve hundred dollars?"

They stare at us with shock, as if we did something really stupid, but we stand our ground. We have a responsibility to defend the actions of our kingdom.

ME: "It was for a good cause."

The Fates look down at their notebooks and scan for their next question. I peek around at the crowd behind them.

ME: "There are other people in line."

I try to sound as polite as I can. Merilee gives me a scowl.

MERILEE: "You have had some altercations with the police. How do you intend to protect the sovereignty of your country?"

CHARLIE: "What's *sovereignty*?"

MERILEE: "Your right to exist."

SAMI: "Public support. People want us to be here."

CHARLIE: "Everybody likes us."

ME: "We offer something special. Our country is a place of complete tolerance."

MERILEE: "Intriguing. Will you allow sun worshipers in?"

ME: "Of course."

MEHRA: "Global warming deniers?"

SAMI: "Yes."

MARCIE: "Refugees?"

SAMI: "Definitely."

MERILEE: "Even if it means jail time?"

SAMI: "Yes."

MARCIE: "Homeless people?"

ME: "They're already here."

I point to the two tents at the bottom of the kingdom. The Fates look over.

MERILEE: "You're a kingdom. Do you have a king?"

We look at each other. We're taking turns but have forgotten whose turn it is.

CHARLIE: "I'm king."

ME: "We take turns."

Merilee looks at Charlie and squints.

MERILEE: "Were you elected?"

CHARLIE: "Yes."

Merilee looks down at her notebook again.

MERILEE: "Are Jews welcome?"

SAMI: "Yes."

MEHRA: "Hindus?"

SAMI: "Yes."

MARCIE: "Muslims?"

ME: "Of course."

MARCIE: "Buddhists?"

CHARLIE: "Yes."

MEHRA: "What about the Dalai Lama?"

ME: "Who's that?"

MEHRA: "The exiled spiritual leader of Tibet."

ME: "Sure."

MERILEE: "What about communism? Would you allow a communist party to form?"

ME: "Yes."

MERILEE: "But what if they cause a revolution in your country and try to take power by force?"

CHARLIE: "Violence is forbidden, so we would kick them out."

MERILEE: "You'd kick them out?"

ME: "Yes."

MERILEE: "You'd use force, then?"

SAMI: "Yes, if we had to."

MERILEE: "And who exactly would exercise that force? Do you have an army?"

Merilee rolls her eyes.

CHARLIE: "So far there's just three in our army, but it will grow when we hire more soldiers."

The Three Fates stare with unbelieving faces. They are not satisfied but have run out of questions. My guess is that they won't ask anything they haven't prepared.

I'm right. After a long stare, they thank us for our time, step out of the line-up, and approach the river. Watching them cross is a sight I will remember for the rest of my life. There's nothing extraordinary about it, but something in the way they step up to the river, stop, and wait, strikes me. It's as if they're waiting for it to stop flowing and part, like Moses at the Red Sea, to allow them to walk across dry land.

It doesn't. They enter the river with their notebooks over their heads. As the water rises to their stomachs, they put their notebooks in their mouths, link hands, and continue crossing. Nature makes no special arrangements for anyone, unless you are Moses.

On the other side, they climb the bank and shake out their dresses. Their clothes stick to them now like wet paper, which makes them look like very skinny wet cats. They walk away faster and faster, never once turning around to look back.

# Chapter 13

TODAY IS A DAY of reckoning.

We return to the kingdom, as we do every day, and clean up the grounds. It is amazing how much garbage people make in a single day. Our goal is to become one hundred percent litter free. We have posted signs in the toilets to ask people to take home whatever they bring to the kingdom, and yet we still find cans, bottles, wrappers, and plastic every morning. We separate the recyclables from the non-recyclables, and bag everything. Then we carry the bags across the river every few days and bring it to my house, where we add it to the city's regular pickup, which we feel is only fair because it came from the city in the first place.

Then we clean the toilets. It's a pretty stinky job but has to be done, and we don't really mind doing it because we are so proud of our kingdom. After that we take a peek at the tiny campground where the homeless people are staying. Everyone is still asleep. Homeless people, we have learned, sleep a lot.

After cleanup and inspections, we take our seats on the Council, sit back and watch as a steady stream of people cross the river and enter the kingdom. Every day there are more, and every day there are more things happening, such as street musicians, jugglers, magic tricks, and acrobatics. It is more interesting every day. Our kingdom has become a centre of fun and entertainment for the whole city. And then, just when we least expect them . . . the police finally show up. This time, it isn't just a couple of officers.

They come down the river in boats. Four rubber dinghies with three or four officers in each one land on the north side of the island. The police step out without getting their feet wet. They are big officers, and look even bigger with their bulletproof vests, billy clubs, and guns. They mean business. They frown at the music, the dancing, the jugglers, and magic tricks. They frown when they see the tents, the toilets, the garden, and flagpole. They talk to some people, who point to us. Then they come over. One of them appears to be in charge. He stands in front of us, breathing heavily, even though he hasn't even done any work.

OFFICER: "Okay, you've had your fun. It's time for you to get off this island."

CHARLIE: "This is our land."

OFFICER: "No, it isn't. This is city property. Get off now or you will be arrested."

SAMI: "This is the Kingdom of No Worries; you have no right to arrest us."

CHARLIE: "Maybe we should arrest you."

The police officer looks very angry.

OFFICER: "You've got ten minutes to grab your stuff and leave."

Everyone around us is watching and listening, and people are coming closer. More people are crossing the river. This makes the police a little nervous, I think, but they are standing their ground. I guess they don't have any choice; this is their job. Suddenly someone in the crowd shouts out, "If you arrest the Council, you'll have to arrest me, too!"

"Me, too!" says another person, and then another.

"You'll have to arrest all of us!"

The police look around. They're surrounded by people but don't look like they are about to change their minds. I don't know what's going to happen. I have a sick feeling in my stomach and I'm wondering if we're going to have a riot. I wonder what our responsibility is if we have a riot in our kingdom. Before that can happen, something else happens, something truly wonderful.

Another boat lands next to the police boats. Out step two men: a big man and a small man. They are dressed in fancy suits. They frown at the police. The police stop what they are doing and stare curiously at the men as they approach. The big man looks like Sami. Then I realize that he is Sami's father. I look at Sami. He's staring at his dad as if he's a Greek god who just came to Earth.

Sami's father wastes no time walking up to the police officer in charge and telling him to back down. On behalf of the Kingdom of No Worries, he has obtained a *court injunction* that prevents anyone from removing the occupants of this river island for thirty days, until the matter can be settled in court. He gestures for his assistant to produce the necessary documents, which he does, pulling some papers out of his briefcase.

The police officer takes the papers, reads the first page, and hands it back. He makes a call on his cellphone, speaks for a while, nodding his head most of the time, then puts his phone away. He gestures with his head to the other police officers, and they start back toward their boats. As he passes us, he points his finger at us and says, "We'll be back in thirty days."

Everyone in the kingdom cheers. Sami is beaming. He follows his dad over to his boat, where they have a private conversation. Then his dad slaps him on the back, gets into the boat with the other man, and they motor away. Sami never takes his eyes off his dad the whole time.

I go to bed tonight happy, thinking of Sami and his dad. Yet something is bugging me, though I don't know what it is. I keep seeing the look on the police officer's face when Sami's dad handed him the papers that granted us thirty days. The officer looked confused at first, then frustrated. I don't know why the police are so determined to get rid of us, except that, well, it's their job, I suppose. But if all the people of Briffin want the kingdom to be here, why won't the police accept it, too? And who will be the one who will ultimately decide anyway? That's what I really want to know.

I get out of bed and sneak into Merilee's room in the hope of asking her just that one question before she falls asleep, but I'm too late. She's snoring like a train engine, and whenever she snores like that, she is impossible to wake up. So I creep back into my room, crawl into bed, and think about it until I fall asleep, too.

In the morning, I ask Dad before he leaves for work. Dad goes to work with a whistle on his lips, like one of the seven dwarfs, because he loves his job. He's in a particularly good mood this morning.

"So, how are things progressing in the kingdom? Should I be calling you King Billy now?" He actually looks unsure if he should or not.

"Pretty good. Sami's father saved us from getting kicked off yesterday. He showed up with something called an injunction."

"No way."

I nod my head.

"He's a lawyer in the Big Smoke, isn't he?" Dad always calls Toronto the "Big Smoke."

"Yeah."

"So he came up here and tied them up for a while, did he?"

"Thirty days."

Dad whistles. "Well, that's going to ruffle a few feathers in City Council."

"Can I ask you a question, Dad?"

"Sure thing. I don't know if I'll be able to answer it, being just a lowly subject myself, but I'll do my best."

"Why, when everyone seems to love our kingdom, and everyone who comes over has a good time, and when we're not bothering anybody, why are the police so angry about it, and so determined to kick us off? Why, when it's such a good thing, do they want to take it away from us?"

"Because, all good intentions aside, you're breaking the law."

"But . . . nobody owned that land before we claimed it."

"Yes, but it sits in the middle of the city, and so the city feels a right to assume ownership of it, and the police are simply the strong arm of the law, acting on the city's behalf. There's nothing personal about it; they simply believe you are breaking the law, which, if they take you to court and prove it, they will have the right to evict you. All Sami's father did for you was buy you some time. Unless you can get a court to grant your kingdom sovereignty, then when those thirty days are up, they will forcibly evict you from the premises. Being twelve years old, I don't think you'll get prison time." Dad smiles. "But some of the people on your island might get arrested. They certainly will if they resist the police."

"But . . . how can the city *feel* the right to assume ownership? The city's not a person, so how can it feel anything?"

"Well, you're right, I suppose. But the city is us, isn't it? It's all of us. And just as you guys are the leaders of your kingdom, the city has to have leaders who make decisions on behalf of the rest of us. Our leaders are duly elected, of course, and so if we don't like the decisions they make, we can change our leadership. That's democracy. But you understand all of that now, right? Merki said you were reading *The Republic*."

"Uhh . . . yeah, sort of."

"Good for you. Remember: the police are only acting on behalf of the City Council, who act on our behalf, and so, crazy as it may seem, the police are just acting in your own best interest when they evict you from where you are not legally allowed to be."

"Okay, I understand that, but it sure doesn't feel like they are acting on our behalf."

"Try not to take it personally. Joe Henderson, the

Chief of Police, is a friend of mine. He's a great guy, but I wouldn't want him to catch me breaking the law."

"The Chief of Police is your friend?"

"Yes. We went to school together, just like you and your friends. I remember him when we used to play on the monkey bars. Come to think of it, he was a stickler for the rules back then, too."

"Oh. Thanks, Dad."

"No worries. I've got to go. We're ripping up Princess Street today, and I don't want to miss it because I was there when it was paved for the first time."

"Okay. See ya, Dad."

"See ya, King Billy."

# Chapter 14

THE SUMMER IS LONG and hot and dry. The river drops a foot and a half, which makes it easier for people to cross. There are even places where people can cross without getting their clothes wet. We're very happy about that because when your clothes get wet every day, your skin gets itchy.

With less water in the river, the kingdom grows by twenty-five percent. That's a lot. But it doesn't take long for the extra land to get covered with plants, animals, and people. Our homeless population swells to five tents, seven people, three dogs, and one rat, because one of the homeless people has a pet rat. There are also two stray dogs who have escaped the city's dog-catcher and made the kingdom their home. They're really friendly, and every day they make the rounds to get petted and fed by hundreds of people.

Our garden grows higher and wider, as people bring over small trees and bushes, which grow very quickly, even though it is a dry summer and the grass above the riverbanks turns yellow. The soil in the kingdom is watered by the river, so the plants here stay green and lush. From a distance it looks like an oasis in the middle of a desert.

There is also a large portable shelter set up, just poles and a tarp, under which a hundred people can sit out of the sun, or two hundred if they squeeze together. Many older people sit there in the shade and read, especially in the mornings, or watch street performers in the afternoons, or listen to concerts in the evenings. The Briffin Bach Society performs every Sunday now because they have become so popular. Their first concert featured "The Four Seasons," music by an Italian composer called Vivaldi. Everybody loved it, even the people who don't like classical music. There's something special about hearing music outside, any music, in the middle of a river.

There's jazz music, too, and rock, disco, and pop. There are singers who sing songs for children, and singers who sing songs for old people.

We have accepted more advertisements, too. People come from other cities to advertise in the kingdom. The portable toilets (there are five of them now) are completely pasted with advertisements on the inside and out. There are ads for roofing, gardening supplies, libraries, churches, laundromats, grocery stores, garages, and almost everything you can think of.

If you add up all the money we have taken in from the very beginning of the kingdom, we have earned six thousand, two hundred and thirty-seven dollars. What we have left is thirty-seven dollars.

One thing we have learned in running our own country: it is a lot easier to earn money than it is to keep it, because the line-up of people looking for money is just as long as the line-up of people who want to advertise. The money goes out just as quickly as it comes in. The Kingdom of No Worries is now the proud sponsor of the Briffin Shelter for Wounded Puppies and Kittens; the Briffin Soup Kitchen; the Briffin Chapter of Amnesty

International; the Canadian Association for the Rehabilitation of Race Horses; the Briffin Lost Child Fund; the Huronia Historical Society; and the Briffin Public Library.

We've had more interviews, too. In fact, there are interviews almost every other day, from faraway places. We've been interviewed by TV reporters from the US, Britain, Germany, France, Spain, Italy, Australia, India, and Japan. Mostly they ask us the same questions, although they sound different in different accents. We've become better at answering them, being kings for a while now. When we are asked why we started the Kingdom of No Worries, our answers sound more like this:

SAMI: "When we look at the world today, we realize that it needs more places where people can live in harmony, equality, and fairness, without fear of oppression."

CHARLIE: "Our dream is to make the Kingdom of No Worries a model country for all the world to see."

ME: "We have learned that people of all walks of life can come together and be happy and joyful and have fun together, even when their interests are different."

SAMI: "We have learned that people everywhere are basically the same, even when they speak different languages, have different coloured skin, eat different food, listen to different music, and wear different clothes. Everyone just wants to be happy and live in harmony."

CHARLIE: "We have learned that you don't need a lot of money to be happy if you are willing to share."

For twenty of the thirty days granted by the injunction, life in the kingdom is blissful. Everyone is happy and the river is a beautiful place to be. Flowers have blossomed everywhere, birds have made nests in the taller bushes and sing in the mornings and evenings, people carry over barbeques, and there is always food for everyone.

But on the twenty-first morning there is a change. I don't know what it is exactly but I can feel it. Maybe it's a small change in the weather, I don't know. It's still hot and dry, but the air seems to carry dampness in the morning and night, like a fine mist, so that it feels as though rain is on its way, even though it isn't in the forecast.

On this morning, long before we normally receive people in the Council, we have a visit by two men who say they have something important to share with us. So, we take our seats in the Council, which is now under a tarp to protect us from the sun. One of the men is holding a folded paper that he opens, holds up, and shows to us. It's a map. He speaks with a husky voice and a native accent. He says he is the chief of a First Nation.

CHIEF: "Good morning. We have come here today to tell you that this island is not your land. This is First Nations land."

Sami, Charlie, and I stare at each other. We are shocked.

ME: "How can it be First Nations land? It wasn't even here before?"

The chief makes a face like a smile, but it isn't really a smile.

CHIEF: "It was here before. Look at this map. This map was drawn in 1837. Here you can see the land that became the city. That is our land, too. Look here and you will see the river run through the city. See in the middle of the river, where we are now. This land was here before. This land is sacred. This was a burial ground for our people. You have no right to be here. This is our land."

CHARLIE: "Let me see that."

Charlie jumps up and stares at the map closely. Sami and I do, too. It's a photocopy of an old map. It's faded and roughly drawn, and hard to make out anything clearly. I see what looks like a river, but I have to squint, and can't see an island in it.

ME: "I don't see it."

The chief nods his head.

CHIEF: "It is our land."

CHARLIE: "This is the Kingdom of No Worries."

CHIEF: "No. This is First Nations land. You have no right to be here."

We don't know what to say. When we ask the men what they think we should do, they say we should leave, and take everyone else with us. We explain that we have a court injunction that gives us thirty days before anyone can move us off the island. They say that doesn't mean anything to them, that we should leave right now.

But we don't want to, so we just sit and stare at the two men for a really long time, which is very uncomfortable. Eventually more people come over, and someone starts playing a guitar, someone lights a barbeque, and people begin working in the garden. Finally the two men turn and leave, but say that they will be back.

As I'm lying in bed trying to sleep, I hear Merilee come upstairs and flop onto her bed. Sometimes she falls asleep with her clothes on. I wonder if other families are like ours. Probably not. I get out of bed and tap lightly on her door.

"What do you want?"

"Can I ask you a question?"

"I should charge you for it; you guys must be worth thousands by now."

I push open the door and enter the darkness of her room. "We were, but we gave it all away."

"Holy crap. Did it ever occur to you that you might need money to run a country?"

"It's really hard to keep money around; there are so many important organizations that need it."

"Who doesn't? Still, you need money to run a country. You should hire a *treasurer*."

"What's a treasurer?"

"Someone who will watch your money for you, so that you don't give it all away."

"Do you know where we could find someone like that?"

"I could do it for you."

"Really? You would?"

"For a fee, of course. Never hire a treasurer who works for free."

"Why not?"

"A treasurer who works for free has no real concept of money. Either that or they're corrupt and stealing behind your back."

"How much would we have to pay you?"

"I don't know. A percentage, I suppose."

"I'll have to discuss it with the Council."

"You do that. What's your question?"

"Some First Nations people came to see us today. They told us we are on their land, and that we have to get off."

"That's probably true."

"What should we do?"

"Either get off, or take it to court. You probably won't win but it ought to buy you at least a couple of decades. If you're still living in your kingdom when you're thirty years old, it'd be a blessing if someone kicked you off."

"But they say it is an old burial ground, and that we are disrespecting their ancestors by being here."

"So . . . show them some respect."

"How?"

"I don't know, invite them to a celebration, invite them to showcase their culture, have a ceremony for the dead, I don't know, I have to get some sleep. Close the door on your way out."

"Okay. Thanks."

"No worries. Let me know if you want me to be your treasurer."

"Okay."

# Chapter 15

ON THE 28TH DAY of our 30-day *immunity* period
(that's what the newspapers call it), we hold a celebration to honour the ancestors of the First Nations people
who have been buried here. We advertise in the paper
but don't really expect many people to notice it. We are
so wrong. It turns out to be the busiest day we've ever
had in the kingdom. In our advertisement, which has
been created by our new treasurer, we have invited anyone with an interest or association with Indigenous culture to come to the kingdom and share their thoughts,

feelings, music, art, stories, and gifts. We are completely overwhelmed with the response.

The day starts early. People who look like they are First Nations, and people who don't, come over with tables, chairs, drums, decorated spears, decorated clothing and start preparing themselves for performances of music and dance.

People bring over pictures and hang them from temporary walls they make out of poles. One corner of the garden becomes a sort of gallery of First Nations art. There are also a couple of storytellers, but they speak so softly, and there's so much noise, and we're so busy, that we never get to hear them.

People from other cultures come, too, and we wonder if they misunderstood our advertisement, because there are people in traditional dress from Africa, India, and South America. The First Nations people don't seem to mind. They just go about their celebration as if they are the only ones there. But each group cooks its own style of food on barbeques and open grills, and the smells that drift across the kingdom are amazing.

Green Daddy's still sends over pizza, though Sami, Charlie, and I never get any anymore because our homeless population has grown so much, and the homeless people are always hungry. They greet the pizza delivery guy as soon as they see him coming across the river.

We watch for the two First Nations men who told us to leave but never see them, although they might have come in traditional dress and we just don't recognize them. The native people wear feathers on their heads and clothes. Their clothes are made of deerskin and are covered with beads.

In the middle of the afternoon, another group of First Nations people come down the river in a birchbark canoe. They're smiling and laughing as they pull the canoe out of the water and join the celebration. There are so many people in the kingdom now you can hardly see beyond walls of smiling faces and waving arms.

In the late afternoon, we recruit a group of volunteers to run around and quiet everyone down so that the First Nations people can hold a ceremony to honour their ancestors. They do this with drums, dancing, and chanting, while thousands watch from the kingdom, and from the riverbanks. Film crews are there to capture everything. It is so amazing.

After the ceremony, there are a few moments of silence in the kingdom, which is really strange considering there are so many people. Somehow that silence, more than anything else I have witnessed all summer long, shows me the power of people when they come together. Because it is easy to make noise with lots of people, but to create silence takes the will of everyone all at the same time. This creates a collective will. When there is a collective will in the air, it creates an energy that you can feel in every molecule of your body. It is a little scary even, because you know that the energy can be used for either good or bad. Today, it is used for good. But if it were ever to turn bad, as in a riot or something, I would be very afraid of it.

The silence is broken eventually by a little talking, laughter, something sizzling on a grill, and the wind. It is then, in the moments immediately after the silence, that I feel the summer change. I don't know what it is exactly but it is in the air, in the wind, and maybe in the dampness. If I were superstitious, which I'm not, I might even say that it is because we have woken the spirits of the people buried where we are standing. And they have woken in a grumpy mood.

The day stretches out to be the longest day in the kingdom, with hundreds of people staying past midnight. Merilee stays, and so do Sami, Charlie, and I, with our parents' permission. A hot haze hangs in the air, the sun goes down in a flash of deep red, and you can feel that a change of weather is coming.

The heat stays long after the sun goes down. It's in the sand and water, like the heat of a hot thunderstorm. But still the rain does not come. A little after midnight my mom and dad come to pick us up, and we give Sami and Charlie a ride home. It's the first time my mom and dad have ever come to the kingdom together. They wander around as if they are visiting an island in the Caribbean. It is so strange to see them here and for them to see us treated as the rulers of our own country.

They see Merilee waiting anxiously for us to make up our minds over a suggestion she has come up with for raising money: a plan in which people can pay five dollars to have their names inscribed on a small wooden footbridge to be built across the river from Briffin to the Kingdom of No Worries.

Merilee has already collected seventy-five dollars, and we haven't even made up our minds yet. But finally we do, and Merilee looks as pleased as when she gets an A+ in school, which she does all the time. Then we squeeze into the car, with Charlie on Sami's lap, and Merilee returns to her old self, telling me that I stink and need to take a bath as soon as we get home. She's right about that, too.

# Chapter 16

THE NEXT DAY, our final day of immunity, is by far the strangest on the island. It's one of those days where, whichever way you turn, you see something weird happening, so that you just kind of wish you could go back home, climb into bed, and stay out of trouble. But we can't. We have a film crew coming. Merilee is arranging for a contractor to give an estimate for building the bridge. The Briffin Bach Society is putting on a special concert with the Briffin Children's Choir, for the Children's Hospital, for which we have promised to clear a space and make sure they have shade and refreshments.

It starts with a dead dog. An old dog floats down the river and washes up on the north side of the island. We discover it when we are making our inspection. Charlie sees it first.

CHARLIE: "What's that?"

ME: "It looks like a blanket."

SAMI: "I don't think it's a blanket; I think it's an animal."

When we get closer, we see that it is a dog.

CHARLIE: "Is it still alive?"

SAMI: "Nope."

CHARLIE: "Can we resuscitate it?"

SAMI: "Nope."

CHARLIE: "Maybe we should try."

ME: "It's dead, Charlie. It drowned."

CHARLIE: "Maybe it's not dead. Maybe it's just sleeping because it's exhausted."

Sami nudges the dog's head with his foot.

SAMI: "It's dead."

ME: "We should bury it."

CHARLIE: "Maybe we should take it to the vet and see what they think."

SAMI: "Charlie, it's *dead*."

Sami nudges its head again, a little harder.

CHARLIE: "Don't hurt it!"

ME: "We can't hurt it if it's already dead, Charlie. We should bury it."

SAMI: "Where?"

ME: "I don't know. Maybe over behind the flagpole."

SAMI: "What will the First Nations people think if we bury a dog on their ancient burial site?"

ME: "I don't know. We don't have to tell them."

CHARLIE: "I think we should take it to the vet."

ME: "Charlie . . ."

CHARLIE: "What?"

ME: "Never mind. I'll get the shovel."

So we dig a hole behind the flagpole, drag the old dog across the ground, and lay it in the hole. Charlie stares at it the whole time, waiting for it to wake up, but it never does. Then we fill in the hole with dirt and stamp down the top.

SAMI: "Everyone will know we buried something here."

ME: "Nobody will ever know, and if they do, we'll just tell them it's compost, 'cause it sort of is."

CHARLIE: "We should tell them the truth. What if somebody's looking for their dog?"

ME: "Oh, yeah. Okay, I guess we'd better tell them the truth."

CHARLIE: "The First Nations people won't mind because they love animals."

ME: "That's true."

SAMI: "Besides, if people discover that we buried a dog without ever telling anybody about it, they might think that we killed it and are trying to hide the evidence."

ME: "What? Nobody will think that; that's crazy!"

SAMI: "They might."

I stare at Sami and Charlie, and we look down. We have dirt on our hands. I look over at the trough we made by dragging the dog across the sand. Then I turn the other way and see three homeless people standing and watching us. They have seen the whole thing. They drop their heads, turn around, and walk silently back to their tents. Suddenly the winds pick up. I have the strongest feeling that this day is going to run out of control.

The Briffin Bach Society comes early. They're nervous about having enough space for the children's choir, even though we promised them they could have the space beneath the large tarp. They start crossing the river with umbrellas and chairs, but the wind begins to gust just when they are halfway across, and their umbrellas open and pull them down the river. One lady's dress blows up over her head, and the wind knocks her over, so that her friends have to rescue her from drowning. Then the wind grabs at their chairs, and most of them turn back to the other shore and just stand and wait for the wind to die down. A little while later they try again, this time succeeding in making the crossing.

The wind howls and wails. It comes in large sudden gusts, and then settles down. It seems that every time anyone wants to do anything, it rises up and tries to blow them down. By the middle of the morning it has blown away three of the homeless tents, and sent their inhabitants into the river to retrieve them. They manage to save only two.

In the afternoon, the film crew arrives. There are hundreds of people in the kingdom now, mostly regular visitors, and a few tourists. People struggle to keep their barbeques under control. Everyone talks about the rain that hasn't yet come.

The film crew is from the CBC. Elizabeth is with them. They have come before but have returned because they know this is our last day of immunity. They want to check in with us. So we take our seats in the Council, stare into the cameras, and answer their questions as best we can. It's a strange feeling knowing that our interview will play in homes all across the country, although they never play the whole thing, just parts of it, and you never know which parts they will play. Sami always gets the most attention because he's the most photogenic. He has movie-star quality.

CBC: "We are happy to visit you boys once again on your river island kingdom. It's quite a blustery day. Did you boys ever think your kingdom would last this long? You've been here what, almost two months now?"

SAMI: "Almost. We knew we would last this long but we never knew we'd get so much attention."

CHARLIE: "Everyone loves us."

CBC: "You have had performances in your kingdom all summer long, and I see the Briffin Bach Society and children's choir setting up right behind us as we speak. Did you ever dream this land would become so popular?"

ME: "No."

CBC: "How do you account for your success?"

SAMI: "Our message of tolerance and equality for everyone."

CBC: "It is an inspiring message, and we have to agree

it works because you have brought thousands of people over to your kingdom, even visitors from other countries, and yet, so far there has been no injury, no hostility, and no violence."

CHARLIE: "We buried a dead dog this morning."

The interviewer smiles awkwardly and ignores Charlie's comment.

CBC: "What about tomorrow? Tomorrow the police will come, and they will have the legal right to remove you from this piece of land. If they do, will you go peacefully?"

Charlie shakes his head.

CHARLIE: "This is our country. They have no right."

SAMI: "We will practise non-violent resistance, like Gandhi."

CBC: "You will let them arrest you?"

SAMI: "Yes."

CBC: "And the others who follow you here; if they intend to come tomorrow, will you advise them to stay away?"

ME: "No. They can do whatever they like. That's what the Kingdom of No Worries is all about; people can do whatever they like."

CBC: "But if those people should clash with the police,

will you take responsibility for that, being the leaders of this kingdom?"

I have no idea how to answer that. Luckily, Sami does.

SAMI: "Let's wait and see what happens tomorrow."

CBC: "But you won't leave?"

SAMI & CHARLIE & ME: "No."

CBC: "And you're willing to go to jail?"

SAMI & CHARLIE: "Yes."

I'm still not sure about that.

CBC: "What advice would you have for other people who might like to follow your example and declare their own country within an existing country?"

ME: "Be welcoming to everyone, and people will respect you."

SAMI: "Don't think nationally; think *globally*."

CHARLIE: "Follow your dreams."

# Chapter 17

WE GO HOME in the darkness, in the middle of a dry thunderstorm. The wind keeps circling the city, bringing the thunderstorm in, and sucking it out, but never really taking it away. It thunders for most of the night, very slowly drifting away as the wind grows weaker and weaker until by morning it is gone. What is left in its place is sticky air, suffocating heat, and an indescribable energy that is uncomfortable. Everyone wishes it would just rain.

For the first time, my mom says she thinks I should

stay home; she doesn't have a good feeling about this day at all. Dad looks the same but doesn't say anything; he just wishes me luck. Merilee is busy drawing up a contract for the bridge builder. She has printed out hundreds of cards for people to write their names on. You can even have your name inscribed on a special metal plate on the floor for fifty dollars if you want, but she hasn't sold any of those yet. Merilee's own take on the bridge project is ten percent. She asked the Council for that, and we agreed.

I walk to the kingdom slowly this day. There's a pop can on the sidewalk, and I kick it all the way to the end of the block before putting it in the recycling. For the first time, I'm not in a hurry to get to the Council. I'm kind of hoping it will rain so hard that everyone will stay home. I feel a lot of anxiety about the police. Sami and Charlie seem to want to go to jail. I don't. If you go to jail when you are just twelve years old, what kind of life will you have?

When I come down the hill, I see that my fears are correct. The police are already here. They haven't come to the island yet, but you can see their cars and vans parked in the middle of the streets that come down to the river. Sami and Charlie are in the kingdom already, sitting in Council. My seat is bare. They must be wondering where I am, so I hurry across the river and join them.

There are a few dozen people in the kingdom, besides the homeless ones who are sleeping in their tents. People are in the garden tending the plants and flowers as if they are in their own backyards. They aren't paying any attention to the police; maybe they haven't even seen them. I have a sickening feeling in my stomach that just won't go away.

CHARLIE: "Where have you been, Billie-Jean?"

SAMI: "We were starting to wonder if you weren't coming."

ME: "Sorry, guys, I'm just kind of slow today. That was quite a storm last night, eh?"

SAMI: "It struck a tree in our neighbourhood."

CHARLIE: "It struck a tree in *our* neighbourhood, too."

ME: "Did you guys see the police vans?"

SAMI: "Yeah."

CHARLIE: "I hope they arrest us."

ME: "What? That's crazy, Charlie. We don't want to get arrested."

CHARLIE: "Yes, we do. That'd be cool. They'd put us in jail and everything."

ME: "Charlie, we don't want to go to jail."

CHARLIE: "Yes, we do."

ME: "No, we don't. That's a stupid idea. Don't you know that all the worst people are in jail? If we go there we'll probably get beaten up and maybe even killed."

CHARLIE: "No, we won't. Everybody loves us."

ME: "Charlie, the people in jail don't even know who we are and wouldn't care if they did."

CHARLIE: "Yes, they do. They have TV in jail, you know, and comfortable sofas and good food. You probably even get your own computer."

ME: "Charlie, I don't think you really understand what jail is."

SAMI: "I think the guys in jail will probably like us because we were arrested, too, and so we're kind of on the same side."

ME: "I don't want to be on the side of criminals."

CHARLIE: "We're not criminals; we're heroes."

ME: "We're not heroes; we're just kids."

Sami stands up and looks around 360 degrees. I watch him watch the people in the garden, the homeless community, and the stray dogs that have made the kingdom their home and are sleeping at the base of the flagpole.

SAMI: "I don't know, I think we're kind of heroes."

There's a trickle of people crossing the river now. I'm surprised. I didn't think anybody would come today. Who wants to get caught in the middle of a fight with the police?

As it turns out: a *lot* of people.

I don't know why the police don't come over right away and tell us to leave before everyone arrives. Wouldn't it be easier to clear the island when there are just a few dozen people on it? Won't it be much harder trying to move thousands? I don't understand that. I don't understand anything.

The morning drags on hot and sticky. It's so muggy the advertisements on the toilets are peeling off. My skin is clammy and I'm constantly wiping my face. It doesn't seem to bother the people in the garden. I have come to realize that gardeners live in their own world. Finally, by noon, the rain begins to fall.

At first it's a soft rain. It falls lightly, like mist, but has the feel of rain that is here to stay. It's hot out, so people don't mind getting wet. But the air is tense, as if it's just waiting for something big to happen, and yet people keep coming.

By the middle of the afternoon, everyone and everything is soaking wet, except for the things that are underneath tarps, but even those are damp. The kingdom is filled to the brim with people, and the sound of drums mixes with the sound of the rain on the tarps and the ground. Barbeques are sizzling and people are shaking out their clothes, and still everyone is happy. But the police have moved their vans closer to the river. They have blocked off parts of the streets. We watch them do that, as if they are preparing for a parade. They do everything slowly, and I keep wondering what they are waiting for.

News vans have also arrived on the riverbanks. Little radars spin around on their tops. The news people start trickling across the river with their umbrellas, chairs, and cameras. They, too, look like they're setting up for a parade. I don't understand why nobody seems afraid of what's coming.

The rain falls harder. People who have been wringing out their clothes stop wringing them and just accept being soaked. I see a couple of the homeless get up and move their tents further from the water's edge, and then I realize something: the river is rising. I look over at the police. They have dogs and horses now but are still biding their time. What are they waiting for?

Without warning, there is a crack of thunder in the

sky. It is so loud, so sharp, and so close it scares the heck out of everyone. The clouds turn black. A storm has arrived.

The rain falls faster. The sky is so dark now we can hardly see the riverbanks. We can't tell what the police are up to. But we can see the lights of their cars flashing. Is that because they are about to invade us, or is it just to warn everyone to be careful of the storm? I don't know.

All along I have been unsure what role the police are playing. Are they here to remove us or simply to protect us? I think they're going to remove us, because that's what they said they would do.

The rain is now just a wall of water, like a tidal wave. I have never seen rain like this before. In the kingdom, everyone is trying to squeeze together under the tarps, but there are too many people and too little space. I can't see our homeless community anymore, but I see a dark figure come to the centre of the island, dragging a tent behind him.

The river is rising fast. How far will it rise before it stops? A few people are making their way off the kingdom now but most are staying. And then, finally, we hear the police over a megaphone.

"Leave the island now! You are not safe! Leave the island now!"

They say this over and over, but no one obeys.

"Leave now," the message repeats, "or you will be forcibly evacuated."

Now they are warning us, but still no one leaves. For another hour or so nothing happens. The rain just pounds the island and river. It knocks down all the tarps and flattens the flowers. We can hardly see outside of the kingdom, but I do see the silhouettes of riders on horses at the river's edge. Then we hear another voice on the megaphone, a frantic voice calling my name. It's my mom.

"Billy! Billy! You must cooperate with the police! The river is too dangerous now! Come home, Billy!" Her voice comes and goes through the rain, but I can tell that she is upset. Then I see a man crossing the river the way we always come, and I recognize him, too. It's my dad. He's in his shorts, the ones he wears around the house, which tells me that Mom has worried him enough to leave without getting properly dressed. He's standing in the river up to his chest, staring at the sky. He's struggling against the current, because it's flowing much faster than before. It doesn't even look like the same river. The police come over the megaphone again, ordering us off the island more urgently.

But there is another sound. A chant. At first, it starts

out small, like the sound of the wind. Then it grows into a thunderous sound. It is the people in the kingdom and on the other shore—thousands of voices raised together. "*We won't leave! We won't leave! We won't leave!*" Sami and Charlie chant, too, and wave their fists in the air.

The police collect into a tight group. They raise shields, turn, and move towards the crowd on the bank. The crowd turns and moves towards the police. A shiver runs up my spine. A riot is about to begin.

# Chapter 18

EVERYTHING HAPPENS so quickly. After watching things move in slow motion for so long, what happens next is hard to follow. First, part of the crowd on the kingdom enters the river to join the crowd on the other riverbank, to confront the police. Police horses enter the water to cut them off, but the river is too high, and the horses have to turn back. I glance at the borders of the kingdom and see them shrinking fast! Water is only metres from the flagpole. Our garden will soon be flooded. But the very worst thing happens next. The crowd that has stepped into the river from the kingdom gets caught in the current and is being swept away.

Within minutes we go from a threatening confrontation with police to a life-threatening disaster. I hear screaming in the river. It's horrible. The words of the CBC interviewer run through my head: "Will you take responsibility for the people?"

How can we take responsibility? How can we do anything? I look over at Charlie.

ME: "Sami! We've got to carry Charlie off!"

CHARLIE: "No! I'm staying!"

ME: "Charlie! You can't swim. You'll drown."

CHARLIE: "I don't care! I'm not leaving the kingdom."

ME: "Sami. We've got to take him off."

But Sami just stands and stares. He can't believe what is happening.

ME: "Sami! Snap out of it! We've got to rescue Charlie!"

Obediently, Sami grabs Charlie and picks him up.

CHARLIE: "Put me down! I'm not leaving!"

He wriggles out of Sami's arms and runs away. I turn around and see people running into the water everywhere, getting caught in the current and swept away. It is a nightmare.

And then I see a policewoman step out of the river

into the kingdom. She isn't wearing a bulletproof vest, or carrying a gun or a shield. She has taken them off to swim across the river. She's carrying a megaphone on a cord around her neck. She runs straight to me.

OFFICER: "You're one of the leaders, right?"

ME: "Yes."

OFFICER: "Quick! We need to save these people. Follow me!"

I follow her to the edge of the water where half of the crowd has entered the river. The other half is standing at the edge, trying to decide whether or not to cross. On the riverbank, the police have regrouped and are quickly ripping off their bulletproof vests and helmets. They're running along the bank and entering the river downstream where people are struggling to get ashore.

OFFICER: "Tell everyone who can swim to swim towards the police. Tell them we will help them. Hurry!"

So I do. I put my mouth to the megaphone and holler.

ME: "This is the Kingdom of No Worries. Those of you who can swim, swim to the police! They will help you. Swim to the police! They will help you!"

I say it over and over, and watch as people do it. They jump into the river and start to swim across. The police meet them halfway. The water is over their heads now.

Many stay in the kingdom because they can't swim.

OFFICER: "Tell the people here to form a group and hold hands."

So I do. The people on the island come together and hold hands as the river rises until we can't see the ground anymore. It covers the plants and bushes, and then they go out of sight. I try to see what is happening in the river but it is almost impossible through the rain and all the commotion. People are crying, and some are praying, but more police officers have come over to the kingdom to help. Now, we are standing up to our chests in water, and still the river is rising.

The current is so strong you can't stand against it; you have to move around, and it keeps pushing us downstream. Sami is holding onto Charlie, and Charlie has his arms wrapped around Sami's neck. Then police boats arrive, and they start picking up all the remaining people. They yell at us to get in. But we shake our heads. We just can't leave. Running through my head is something my dad used to say: that a captain goes down with his ship. That's how Sami, Charlie, and I feel. But a strong hand grabs my arm and I turn around to see my dad. He's wearing a sympathetic look on his face. "It's gone, Billy. It's gone."

I can't tell if I'm crying or not because the rain is splashing down on my face. I look at Sami's and Charlie's faces. They look the same as me. "It's gone, guys," I say.

They just drop their heads. Then my dad takes Charlie out of Sami's arms, and the four of us make our way, half walking, half swimming, across the river. It takes us downstream quite a ways before we reach the shore.

When we climb out and walk back up the bank, there is nothing left of the kingdom but the flagpole, its flag hanging down. It looks so defeated. We stand and stare for a long time because it is such a strong image.

Then even the flagpole starts tilting in the direction of the current. Slowly it bends to the river's will until it is flat on top of the water. Then the river carries it away. Now, there is nothing in front of us but a river, just as it had been before, except bigger. The Kingdom of No Worries is no more.

# Chapter 19

THE RIVER DROPS again but not to its former self. It never shows land again, because the old dam upstream has been destroyed by the storm, and they don't believe they need to rebuild it. An increase in the number of factories and treatment plants in the past twenty-five years has lowered the level of the river, except during rainstorms like the one we just had, which doesn't happen every year, and doesn't have any lasting impact on the river's flow to Lake Ontario. So the kingdom is gone and will never be again.

Sami, Charlie, and I have a hard time accepting this at

first, and we meet as the Kingdom of No Worries Council in *exile*, with plans for the future of our country. We have this discussion in my tree fort, in the midst of a junk-food feast, purchased with the kingdom's last remaining revenue: seven dollars. This is all that is left after our treasurer returned the money to the bridge supporters and took her own fee of twenty dollars. True to her word, she was not willing to work for free.

Unlike the kings in the Council, the treasurer has no problem accepting that the kingdom is gone, and she happily returns to school for the remaining two weeks of summer break. She does give me one valuable gift, however, although I believe she does it unknowingly.

We're all sitting in the living room of our house: Dad, Mom, Merilee, Mehra, Marcie, Sami, Charlie, and me. We pile on top of the sofas and the floor, and are watching about two hours of interviews that Dad has put together from TV news footage, interviews of the Council from the very beginning, right to the day of the storm.

It's fascinating to watch, and especially amazing to see how the kingdom grows over the course of a month and a half, from a trickle of people and a few small plants, to thousands of people enjoying themselves on a lush, nearly tropical island filled with music and dance.

It's also interesting to see how the confidence of the

Council grows in all this time, from sounding like three neighbourhood kids to something like world leaders. But the gift Merilee gives me, which means more to me than almost anything else this summer, is simply the word she says as she gets up with the other Fates and leaves the room. As she passes me in the doorway, she stares me in the eye with her eagle look and simply says, "Impressive." If ever there were a time I felt I was wearing a crown, this is it.

Sami, Charlie, and I are meeting this afternoon at Sami's house to play *Demon Revival X*. Sami says there'll be no one home. I believe it. We're going to play until our eyes are bulging. But we also have an appointment downtown this evening. We're not sure to show up as the Council or just ourselves. It's in an old house in a dingy corner of the city. But we're excited to go.

We've been told there is a plaque there on the wall with our names on it, and the "Kingdom of No Worries." That will be fun to see. But what we're even more excited to see, especially Charlie, are the occupants of the house, because we feel a special connection to them. They are the animals of the Briffin Shelter for Wounded Puppies and Kittens. We know they will be happy to see us. As a gift, we thought we would bring them a potted plant.

# Epilogue

NOW I THINK I know who owns the land. Nobody. I was starting to think it was everyone, but I don't think that's true. The land belongs to nobody, just as it always has. Sure, we might use it for a while—plant trees and gardens, build houses and cities, create democracies and kingdoms, with all kinds of laws and rules—but I don't think we can ever really own it. We will come and go, and then other people will come and go, but the land will still be here. In fact, the one thing we learned more than anything else was that you don't take possession of land so much as it takes possession of you.

We started out as kings of our own country and ended up becoming its servants. Not that we minded; it's an awesome feeling being king to thousands of people. But it really just means that you become their servant, because it's a heck of a lot of work, and there are so many responsibilities you hardly have time for anything else. Plato said that a king must be a philosopher, but I think maybe he should have said that a king must be a servant. That would make more sense to me.

But I'd still like to read his book. It must be good if people are still reading it thousands of years after he wrote it, after so many kingdoms have come and gone. That sort of proves Merilee right, that the pen is mightier than the sword. If that's the case, then it's kind of hard to avoid a certain logical conclusion: that to accomplish all of the things we were hoping to accomplish with our kingdom—to make the world a fairer, more equal, and more tolerant place for everyone—we might do a better job by writing a book. Now that's a scary idea. I think I'd better call the Council together for a meeting.

# ABOUT THE AUTHOR

Philip Roy divides his time between two places with his family and cat: his hometown of Antigonish, Nova Scotia, and his adopted town of Durham, Ontario. Continuing to write adventurous and historical children's novels focusing on social, political, environmental, and global concerns, Philip is now learning to illustrate his own books. He is also studying French, and looks forward to having all of his books translated into the French language. Along with writing, travelling, running, composing music, and crafting folk art out of recycled materials, Philip spends his time with his family. Visit Philip at www.philiproy.ca.